STO✓

BOOKS BY BARBARA CORCORAN

A Dance to Still Music
The Long Journey
Meet Me at Tamerlaine's Tomb
A Row of Tigers
Sasha, My Friend
A Trick of Light
The Winds of Time
All the Summer Voices
The Clown
Don't Slam the Door When You Go
Sam
This Is a Recording
Axe-Time, Sword-Time
Cabin in the Sky
The Faraway Island
Make No Sound
Hey, That's My Soul You're Stomping On
"Me and You and a Dog Named Blue"
The Person in the Potting Shed

The
PERSON
in the
POTTING
SHED

BARBARA CORCORAN

The

PERSON

in the

POTTING

SHED

ATHENEUM 1980 NEW YORK

LIBRARY OF CONGRESS CATALOGING IN PUBLICATION DATA

Corcoran, Barbara.
The person in the potting shed.

SUMMARY: While vacationing with their mother and new stepfather
in a semi-deserted plantation house
outside New Orleans, a boy and a girl discover
a murder and help track down the murderer.
[1. Mystery and detective stories] I. Title.
PZ7.C814Pe   [Fic]   80-12299
ISBN 0-689-30774-8

TO
Rachel & Anthony Tuck
with love

2103765

I would like to thank

H ELEN M AR G OULD

for lending me her copy of
"Plantation Parade" by Harnett T. Kane,
and for once having prowled
the plantation country with me.

The
PERSON
in the
POTTING
SHED

1

IT WAS GOING TO BE a strange summer. Both my brother Franklin and I had been at boarding school and had not seen each other since Christmas, which in itself was unusual because we were only a year apart and had always been very close. Also we were about to be reunited with our mother, whom we had not seen for more than a year, fifteen months to be exact. And plus all that, we were to meet our new English father. *And* we were to spend the summer in some weird plantation mansion somewhere on a bayou south of New Orleans. When you consider that we are native New Englanders from Massachusetts, it was certainly going to be different.

The reason for all this was that fifteen months ago when our parents were in England for a conference, they were in a car crash and our father was killed. Our mother was in a London hospital with a broken leg, internal injuries, and shock, and when she got out, she went into severe depression. My aunt went over and stayed with her for many months, and we stayed first with our grandmother and then at boarding schools, Franklin in New Hampshire and I in Connecticut.

When my mother was better, our aunt came home but my mother stayed on in England; and then a couple of months ago we heard from Mother that she had married an Englishman and was bringing him to meet us. At first it was a terrible shock, it seemed so sudden; but Aunt Maggie said he was a wonderful man and it had been the salvation of our mother, so we were glad about that. Mom wrote us long, happy-sounding letters, instead of the sad little notes she'd been sending, and she said we would love Ian. He was brilliant, she said, and he played fantastic tennis.

So my brother and I were on the plane en route to New Orleans, where Mother and her new husband would be waiting for us at the airport. I think we both had very mixed feelings about it all, mostly nervousness.

On top of all that, I was having trouble getting used to my brother. He is a year younger than I am, and he had always been smaller; but suddenly he was about four inches taller, his shoulders were a mile wide, and his voice had changed.

[4]

"What are we supposed to call this man?" he said.

I had wondered myself. "I don't know."

"Mr. Staniford-Jones?" He shook his head. "Somehow I can't think of my mother as Mrs. Staniford-Jones." He gave me an anxious look. "He won't expect us to call him Dad, will he?"

"Of course he won't. Aunt Maggie said he's a very sensitive, sympathetic man. We'll just ask Mother what we should call him. Probably Ian. That's his name, after all."

Franklin stared out the window awhile. "I don't really understand why we're going to Louisiana. What's in Louisiana?"

"Franklin, I told you. Mr. Staniford-Jones teaches architecture or something, and he's going to be a visiting professor at Tulane for a year. Tulane is in New Orleans."

"I know that much."

"He's interested in studying some of the old plantation houses south of New Orleans." I took a Coke from the flight attendant, and after a long indecision Franklin took orange juice. "So somebody at Tulane told him about this rundown plantation where the descendants still live and rent out part of it."

"Sounds charming. Mildew and mold, I suppose, spiders, roaches, snakes. Nothing to do. Boredom."

"Don't be so negative. It sounds like the perfect

place to meet Frankenstein, or at least a corpse or two." At that I knew he was really interested. He was cracking his knuckles, which he does when he's excited. It's a revolting habit. So I decided to settle him down. After all, he was probably right about the boredom. "Do you want part of my candy bar?"

"No."

"Well, don't jump down my throat. I haven't seen you since Christmas. I should think you'd be glad to see me."

"I am, but you talk so much, you make my head ache. You didn't used to talk so much." He turned his head to examine me. "And you look different."

"How?" It's interesting but also scary to be told you look different. You wonder if the self that's familiar to you is slipping away.

"Your face is longer. Your eyes are bigger. They're a different color. They used to be gray, now they're green."

I got my pocket mirror to look. "I don't think it's possible for eyes to change color after infancy. Or size either."

"Why do you always contradict me?"

I sighed. If it was going to be that kind of summer, who needed it?

"And you're shorter. You've shrunk."

"I have not."

Suddenly he grinned, his old flashy smile that lit

up like somebody turning a light on. "You're not really smaller. I'm bigger. Have you noticed?"

"Have I noticed! I've got a kink in my neck from looking up to you."

We took some candy from the cabin attendant's tray. It's supposed to keep your ears from popping when you start the descent. "We're almost there." My stomach tightened up in knots.

Franklin took a deep breath. "Mom says he plays a super game of tennis."

"Dad did, too."

"Well, he's not Dad."

"I know that, but he could be a little like him." A picture of my father flashed into my mind. He had been 5′11, 155 pounds, all muscle. He had curly black hair, like Franklin's, and gray eyes that sometimes looked stern. The pain of missing him shot through me as if someone had punched me in the stomach, and I hardly noticed the descent until I felt the bump of the plane on the ground.

Franklin and I looked at each other and then quickly away. He undid his seat belt too soon and got scolded by the flight attendant. He scowled and set his jaw.

"Did you see the Mississippi?" he said.

"How could I? Your head was in the way."

"You weren't looking. Anyway it looks muddy."

We stood up and got into the slow-moving line,

and I thought I was going to faint or something. I tried to remember exactly what my mother looked like and couldn't. In my mind I could see her bending over my bed when I was little, but she was just a dark outline. Would her breakdown have changed her? When one person dies, does the person who was very close to him sort of die, too, and turn into someone else? If only we could step off the plane and see Mom and Dad standing there waiting for us.

Franklin looked down at me and said in alarm, "Don't cry, for God's sake."

"Who's crying?" I bit my lip hard and turned my face away so he couldn't see me.

We got out of the runway, or whatever it's called, and my ears were crackling; I could hardly hear anything.

"There she is," Franklin said, and I could tell he was as scared as I was.

Our mother was standing on tiptoe, shading her eyes (Against what? There's no sun in the New Orleans airport. Against the sight of us?), and then she saw us. I could see her say, "Oh!" and she looked frightened for a moment and then ran toward us. She looked smaller, shorter than I am and a lot shorter than Franklin is now.

But her voice was the same. There was that little break it gets when she's excited or moved. "Dorothy! Franklin! I can't believe it! You're so big."

"Franklin's big," I said. "I'm not very."

She hugged me hard and turned to Franklin. He looked so forbidding that for a moment she seemed afraid to hug him, but then she did, and she was laughing and crying a little. "Frankie, you've grown so. I hardly knew you."

Unsmiling he said, "That's all right." As if he was a chance acquaintance excusing her for not remembering him, but he was just nervous.

She seemed kind of shaken, and her voice cracked again. "I have someone for you to meet."

I looked up with great expectations. But there was no one there who looked like Dad. Ian was tall and skinny, with a big Adam's apple, and he wore a white shirt and dark tie and carried a tweed jacket slung over his shoulder. He had a small moustache and horn-rimmed glasses. He was smiling, but he looked nervous. He was nice; he just wasn't my father.

"Children, this is Ian," she said, grabbing my arm. "Ian, this is Dorothy, and this enormous young man is Franklin."

We shook hands.

Ian said, "My word, what smashing young people. I'd no idea they'd be so grown up." He had a high voice and an English accent like the BBC commentators on public radio. I'd always thought that only actors and media people spoke that way. It didn't sound real.

[*9*]

My mother chattered a lot while we waited for our luggage, and Ian smiled, and we just sort of stood there. I felt like a piece of excess baggage myself. I felt awfully sorry for Ian, stuck with two kids he didn't even know. Mom should have sent us to Grandma for the summer. I wondered if it was too late to suggest it.

They had been in Louisiana a week already, and when we went out to their rented station wagon, Mom told us some about the place. It was hard to listen to her because there was so much noise and confusion, and the air was steaming. I couldn't believe it was that hot already, not even July yet.

Mom pulled me into the back seat with her, leaving Franklin up front with Ian, which was a tactical error, because when Franklin is unnerved, he freezes up and just doesn't talk at all. He slumped down in his seat and stared straight ahead while Ian tried to make conversation. Now and then Franklin said, "Yes, sir," or "No, sir," as if Ian were his headmaster. I could see the back of Ian's neck getting pink. It wasn't his fault he wasn't anything like our dad.

I could tell that Mom was half listening to the talk in the front seat, even while she talked a blue streak to me. But in time Ian gave up trying to converse with Franklin.

Everybody was driving like mad along the Airline Highway, cutting in and out. "Like Rome," Ian said, suddenly. Driving like a bat out of hell, my dad would have said. Mother was very tense, and I really felt sorry for her.

Suddenly Franklin said, "Look! That can't be."

I looked and saw what he meant. There was the river, and a steamboat was moving slowly along, but the astounding thing was that the ship was higher than we were.

Ian laughed and went into a long explanation about levees and floods and all. I didn't care so much about the explanation, but I did like seeing that boat. And others came along after it. As far as I could tell, they were silent, and it was like watching a parade of ghost ships.

"That's really something," I said, and my mother relaxed a little.

Pretty soon we crossed the river on a high arched bridge, and Ian told us how Louisianans say "parish" instead of "county." Not too gripping a piece of news.

But on the basis of our interest in the levees, Ian plunged into a new role as tour guide. We were coming into the bayou country, he informed us, where a hundred-and-some years ago the French had sugar and cotton plantations for a couple of hundred miles.

"You couldn't go down the river on a boat," he said, his accent getting even more British because he was excited about his topic, "without seeing one great plantation house after another, spreading out farther than the eye could reach. Tremendous houses, built in the neo-Greek manner mostly, some of them with sixty or seventy rooms, and each house had its collection of lesser buildings, from the garçonnière down to the slave quarters."

Mom asked Franklin if he knew what a garçonnière was, which of course he didn't, and she said it was a separate house where the boys lived as soon as they were Franklin's age. "They could come and go as they wished."

Franklin twisted around and gave Mom the first smile since he'd met her. "Hey, cool. They didn't have to tell their mothers?"

"No." She leaned forward and squeezed his shoulder, but that was a mistake. She had overreacted. Franklin turned away again. Mothers, I've noticed, are apt to be like that: give them an emotional inch and they'll take a mile.

Ian was talking away about Greek pediments and ionic columns and pigeon cotes and friezes, but he lost me. I wondered why he was trying so hard. I shut off my mind and just looked.

We couldn't see the river now, and the vegetation on both sides of us was really tropical. Even this early in the summer there were all kinds of flowers—white ones, yellow ones, red ones, trees with bright red flowers—everything kind of overlapping on everything else. The big trees were hung with what Mom said was Spanish moss. It looked like a shroud or something, though I'm not one hundred per cent sure that I know what a shroud is. Anyway it hung in heavy gray veils, like something dead. Mom said it eventually killed the trees, and Ian said politely that he didn't think so.

"It's an epiphyte, actually, an air plant, and a great collector of moisture. Member of the pineapple family."

Pineapple family? The man was putting us on. I could see the back of Franklin's neck stiffen, and I read his mind. We were back to our old habit of thinking the same thoughts at the same time, without a word being spoken. That at least was reassuring.

The station wagon was air conditioned. If it hadn't been, I think we would have expired. You could *see* the heat, in undulating waves. And the windshield was solid bugs. Every few minutes Ian had to push the thing that squirts windshield cleaner and run the wipers. Great country! And yet I couldn't help paying attention to it. It was about as far from New England as the Land of Oz.

Ian was talking about the grand style in which the planters and their families lived. When that man began to talk, there was no shutting him off. ". . . powdered wigs," he was saying, "fabulous jewels, beauty spots on the ladies' faces, great balls."

"Out here in the boonies?" Franklin said in a skeptical tone.

"That's what makes it so fascinating," Mom said. "Out here, as you say, in the boonies, this fantastic French civilization. The men held grants of thousands of acres. They brought their furniture from France, laces, tapestries . . ."

"Who did all the work?" I said.

"Slaves. Hundreds and hundreds of slaves."

"I don't believe in slavery," Franklin said in a disapproving voice, and both Mom and Ian laughed. The back of Franklin's neck reddened. "I mean *ever*," he added.

We turned into a wide drive that had enormous oak trees along each side, like a canopy. I caught my breath, because it really was beautiful.

"We are approaching Belle Rêve, our wee summer cottage," Mom said, and laughed like her old self. I wished I could tell her not to worry about us. If she was happy, we were happy.

2

IT WAS UNBELIEVABLE. There was this house, called
Belle Rêve, that looked like the Parthenon or something, two tall stories high, topped by a triangular
gable that Ian said was called a pediment. Six Corin-
thian pillars went all the way up to the pediment, and
there was an upstairs balcony that ran the width of
the house. The windows, upstairs and down, were
covered floor to ceiling with shutters. (Jalousies, I
later found out, is the word.) On each side of the
house a one-story addition was connected to the
main house by a breezeway. The house had fourteen
rooms.

We had rented the main part of the house, although some of the rooms were closed off. The owner
lived in one of the additions, and the other one was
closed.

The minute you stepped inside, you were almost knocked over by the smell of mildew and damp.

"It's never hot in here," Mom said, "no matter how warm it is outdoors."

I could believe it. It was like walking into a deep freeze. Ian took us on a tour. Downstairs there was an enormous parlor full of old furniture, some of it good, but most of it just plain ugly. The dining room was almost as big, with a strange-looking table that would seat at least thirty people. It was more a setting for Count Dracula than for Frankenstein.

"I see cozy little suppers coming up," Franklin said.

Ian laughed and said he and Mom had been eating mostly in the kitchen. There was a library with matched sets of books by people like Bulwer-Lytton and Charles Reade and a lot of authors I had never heard of. There was "the little parlor," bigger than our living room at home. And we went through a large place, called a butler's pantry, to the kitchen.

"Hey, we could set up a bowling alley here," Franklin said.

The stove must have come over with the first Frenchmen who built the place. It was a big iron thing, a wood stove. Somebody had hooked up a little gas stove next to it, which didn't look too clean. In fact, nothing looked clean. The linoleum on the floor was cracked, and black along the cracks. The refrigerator, which could have been the first one Frigidaire ever made, leaned sideways and badly needed washing. Obviously the slaves were sorely missed.

My room was at the head of the stairs, and it was about the size of a small dance hall. A high four-poster stood in the middle of the floor, with a cheesecloth canopy arrangement to keep out mosquitoes. There were no window screens. The room also opened onto the outside balcony, which Mother said was called a gallery.

After I was left alone, I went out on the gallery. It was a really spooky place. All kinds of bushes and vines grew right up the side of the house, and with all that Spanish moss hanging from the trees, it looked as if the whole outdoors was set up for a funeral.

Franklin came by to tell me his room had a tilted floor. "I wish I had a skateboard." And he said you had to be explicit about the bathroom, because there was one room with a tub on claw feet, "big as a swimming pool," and another room at the other end of the hall that was what Ian called "the loo." Franklin said, "There are festoons of spiderwebs in the loo, full of dead bugs. Did you ever stop to think how efficient a spider is?"

I didn't want to consider the spider just then. "What do you think of him?"

"Him? Oh, he's all right, I guess. It's just that . . ."

"I know. But we should be nice to him, for Mom's sake."

"So who's not nice?"

"You could talk a little more."

"You're the family talker. I'm the silent type."

Later Ian took us on a tour of the other buildings. First there was the garçonnière, set back from the house under some gigantic oak trees. It was brick and octagonal, with a roof like a Chinese pagoda. Franklin was all for moving in, until he stepped inside and got a faceful of cobwebs and dirt. It hadn't been used for years, and it smelled awful. Everything everywhere seemed to be in a state of advanced decay. It made you wonder what kind of people lived here. So far I hadn't seen any other human beings, though I had the eerie feeling that we were being watched.

We looked at a separate two-story brick building that had been the kitchen. Ian said the gentry didn't like to smell the cooking, so the slaves cooked out there and carried the food to the house in covered dishes.

Franklin looked at it and said, "If you can't stand the heat, stay out of the kitchen."

Ian looked so baffled, I thought I should explain; but after I did, although he thanked me politely, I could tell he still didn't get it. I remembered Mom writing us that he was brilliant. Maybe the English show their brilliance in different ways. Actually he was probably suffering from culture shock.

We were walking back to the main house when I had a sudden glimpse of movement in the brush. Was there really someone watching us? I hoped so.

"Who's that?" I said.

"Where?"

"Someone or something just went scuttling through the bushes in back of the garçonnière."

Neither Franklin nor Ian had seen anything. "You're seeing ghosts already," Franklin said. "Your imagination is working overtime."

But I knew something had been there. I didn't really believe in ghosts; but in a place like this, it would be easy to change your mind. "Did they torture their slaves?"

Ian looked surprised. "Oh, I shouldn't think so."

He showed us the gardens, very rundown, overgrown and weedy, and a place he called the potting shed, full of clay pots and garden tools.

"It looks recently used," I said.

"Yes. There's a chap named François who makes a stab at keeping up the gardens."

"It looks as if he whittled rather than stabbed," Franklin said.

I laughed. I happen to think Franklin is witty, though not everyone agrees.

Then we came to the slave quarters. They were bigger than I had expected. A long row of two-story brick houses, each with two doors like a duplex. Ian patted the brick wall and said the slaves were superb craftsmen. "These will never fall down."

One of them looked lived in. When Franklin went up to the door, Ian said quickly, "Better not, old chap. I think the gardener hangs his hat in there."

Franklin looked slightly annoyed, and later he said, "If he meant the gardener lives there, why didn't he say so? Can't he say anything straight out?"

On our way back we came to a carved white iron bench under a tree. The hanging moss almost hid it from us, but as we got close, we saw a woman sitting there. When she saw us, she jumped up as if she were frightened. And I jumped, too. She looked like a witch.

Ian said, "Good afternoon, Miss Eva. Our children have arrived."

Franklin and I shot a look at each other. "Our children" indeed!

"Oh," the woman said, looking like some kind of scared animal. She was very tall and very thin, with long lank hair. She had on a pair of paint-streaked jeans that were too short for her and a boat-necked blouse that kind of hung to one side. Her eyes were enormous and very dark, like a deer's.

"This is Dorothy," Ian said, "and this is Franklin." To us he said, "This is Miss Eva DuPré."

She nodded jerkily and said, "Hi."

It seemed incongruous. In that setting, with that name, I thought at least she would say, *"Bon jour."*

"Your place is very interesting," Franklin said.

"Thanks." She nodded again and took off.

"Miss DuPré is rather shy," Ian said.

It was eerie. In just a second she had disappeared completely, as if she had become disembodied.

"An ancestor of hers was the official welcomer when LaFayette came here," Ian said.

Franklin stared at him in obvious disbelief. "You mean *the* LaFayette?"

"Yes. Quite. He spent some time here."

Franklin thought it over. "Well," he said, "there's a house in our town where George Washington is supposed to have danced in the ballroom. But personally I never believed it."

Ian gave his little scream of laughter. "You are a skeptic, I see."

"You bet your boots."

When I went back up the stairs to my room, I noticed something I'd missed the first time, though it was hard to miss. Right at the head of the stairs was

[*21*]

a life-size painting of a young woman. Franklin caught up with me when I was looking at it.

"That's our Jasmine," he said.

"Jasmine who?"

"How do I know?" He pointed to the printing at the bottom of the painting. It said, "JASMINE, on her debut, 1916." The artist's name was slashed on in one of those fancy signatures you can't read.

This Jasmine was wearing one of those weird evening dresses of that period, with a square neck and puff sleeves and lots of frills and lace and ribbons. She was sitting on a red velvet covered chair, holding one long-stemmed red rose, and leaning a little forward so that her head looked out of proportion to the rest of her. A dark red velvet cape was arranged over the arm of the chair. It didn't look to me like a very good painting, except for the eyes, which absolutely riveted you. She seemed to be looking right into your soul. But on the whole, Jasmine was ordinary looking, not pretty. Her nose was too long, her mouth too small and tight, her cheeks too pulled in, but those eyes were certainly not ordinary.

"She looks like a teenage witch," Franklin said.

"Are there teenage witches?"

"I suppose so. They have to start some time. Hey, look at that chandelier."

The chandelier was beautiful. A whole bunch of crystal drops like tear drops, set in layers, and where the chain went into the ceiling was a big crystal medallion. No wonder Ian was impressed with the place. It was an architect's dream. But it wasn't my dream. Already I was counting the days till we would leave.

Dinner was early, supposedly out of deference to our jet lag, so we could get a good night's sleep.

We didn't expect much of a meal. Under the best of circumstances, our mother is no gourmet cook. She likes to paint, and usually she's off with her painting gear and forgets to start anything for dinner till it's too late, so we end up with something canned or frozen. But it turned out that Ian was doing the cooking. Franklin gave me a withering look when I told him Ian had cooked dinner. Franklin is at a male chauvinist stage, and any man who cooks or knits or cleans the house or whatever Franklin considers "women's work" is an object of contempt. He muttered under his breath that he wouldn't eat a bite, but he did. It was a very good dinner. Ian did his shopping in New Orleans, and he had a Creole cookbook. We had pompano en papillotte, which is a fish in a paper bag, and yellow rice, fresh black-eyed peas, and hot biscuits. It was amazing that he could have done all that in that stupid little stove. I said so, and he looked pleased. Mother beamed.

Later Franklin and I sat on the gallery outside my room, swatting mosquitoes. We were bathed in

[23]

insect repellent, a smell I really hate.

"There's not even a shower in this dump," he said.

"So take a bath. It won't kill you."

"Girls take baths. Men take showers."

"Oh, bull. I heard Ian running a tub before dinner."

"He's English."

"Oh, stop being hostile."

"I am not hostile." His mouth trembled, and I realized he wasn't disliking Ian, he was missing Dad. I tried to sound nicer. "We'll explore the plantation in the morning. Maybe there's something fascinating. If nothing more macabre turns up, maybe at least Jean Lafitte buried some treasure here."

"Oh, sure." But I could see that the idea intrigued him. He left after a while, and I went to bed. I was almost asleep when Mom came in to kiss me good night.

"I've missed you so," she said.

"I missed you too."

"I know you did. Your letters helped preserve what little sanity I had left." She smoothed my hair.

"It must have been very frightening."

"More frightening than I ever dreamed life could be." She paused. "I was driving, you know, at the time of the accident. I hadn't really gotten used to driving on the left. Your father didn't want me to do it, but I insisted. My reflexes just weren't quick enough." Her voice sounded suddenly harsh with self-blame.

"Mom, you can't think of it that way.

"I thought of nothing else for months. Literally. If I hadn't been so pigheaded . . ."

"Don't."

"I thought I was going mad." She took a deep breath. "Then I met Ian." Her voice changed. "He is the kindest, most understanding person I've ever met. Oh, darling, try to like him."

"But I do like him."

"He thinks you don't, either of you." Tears filled her eyes.

"Mom, we like him fine. We just have to get used to him. Like he has to get used to us. I mean he's not . . ."

". . . not your father. I know." She leaned over and kissed me. "Keep your mosquito net snug or you'll be eaten alive."

"Do you suppose slaves stood by the beds and fanned away the mosquitoes?"

She smiled. "I don't know. Sleep well, dear."

But I couldn't get to sleep. Long after Mom and Ian had gone to bed, I thought I heard someone on the stairs. There were loud creaks, but I was too scared to look. The creaks came closer to my room. I pulled the sheet up around me and closed my eyes.

But I couldn't close my ears. Fortunately, in a little while the steps seemed to recede. It wasn't till morning that I was able to think rationally about it. I mean, old houses do creak.

3

WHEN WE GOT UP, Mother had already gone out to
paint the river, which Ian said was about a mile away.
She'd left us one of her notes with funny faces drawn
on it, the way she used to when we were little. The
paper bags we took our lunch to school in were always covered with wonderful little drawings. Ian
gave us our breakfast and then took off with his
camera to photograph some of the architectural details
of the house. When we went out, we saw him hanging over the edge of the roof, on his stomach, trying
to get a close shot of a carved wooden angel. Poor
old Ian. He did work hard at everything.

We walked past the wing where Eva lived. She
wasn't in sight, but a gnarled old woman was hanging
clothes on a line behind the house. She gave us a nod,

not too friendly; but I'm always curious about people so I went over to her.

"Good morning," I said.

" 'Allo." She didn't smile or stop hanging up the sheets.

"Is Miss Eva around?"

She took a clothespin out of her mouth and said, "Gone to work."

"Oh. Does she work somewhere?"

She looked as if she would rather do practically anything than chat with me, but she said, "She work in de bookshop in N'Orleans." She had a strong French accent.

"Oh," I said. "I didn't know that. That's nice. I like bookshops."

"Come on," Franklin said impatiently.

"My name is Dorothy," I said. "This is my brother Franklin." Since she didn't answer, I said, "What is your name?"

"Felicité." She gathered up a whole armful of wet sheets, hugging them to her chest, and went down to the end of the clothesline where she couldn't hear me. I took the hint.

"Friendly type," Franklin said.

"The French are reserved," I said.

"Yeah? How many French do you know?"

I ignored his question. There's no point in answering questions that are not intended to get infor-

mation. We walked along till we came to the garçonnière, which obviously fascinated my brother. He
braved the cobwebs and went inside. His voice
sounded hollow. "This could be really cool if it was
cleaned up."

I went in. There was nothing there but an old
broken oil stove, a broken chair, and litter. "I can see
you living here."

"I said if it was cleaned up. If you had a bunch
of slaves to keep it in good shape . . ."

"I thought you didn't like slavery."

"Well, I don't. I'm saying if you lived then and
didn't know any better." He changed to a less argu-
mentative tone. "Have you noticed something
funny?"

"Lots of things. Which one are you referring
to?"

"There aren't any black people here."

"Maybe you haven't heard of the Civil War."

"Oh, don't be so smart. There are black people
all over the South. We saw them yesterday, all over
the place. Why aren't there any here?"

"Maybe Eva can't afford them."

"She's got that old white woman hanging out
clothes."

"Maybe it's her mother." But I was joking. I had
wondered myself why there were no blacks, but I
assumed Eva couldn't afford help.

I pried Franklin loose from the garçonnière finally, and we went to explore the cook house. It wasn't very thrilling. Some shelves, some cupboards, the wreck of an enormous stove, a huge fireplace, the kind you could cook in, a few rusted pans, an earthenware jug, and a couple more of the big dirty cotton bags that Ian said had been sugar bags. I guess he meant for putting the sugarcane in when it was picked.

We walked along the path past the slave houses. It was very still and humid, and there was a smell of rotting things. Suddenly, close to us, there was a loud noise like a belch. I wanted to run, but I was too scared to move. Talking about ghosts and witches was one thing. Having scary things happen was another. Then Franklin laughed and pointed to the doorway of the house where Ian had said the gardener lived. A gnarled little old man leaned against the doorframe.

"Are you François?" Franklin said.

The old man belched again, jabbed a dirty finger against his chest, and said, "Moi, I am François." He hiccuped.

We watched him lurch down the path to the potting shed, with a funny sidewise walk as if one leg were longer than the other. He went into the shed and slammed the door.

"What's wrong with him?" I said.

"For one thing, he's drunk as a skunk."

"Do you think they really call that the potting shed? It sounds more English than French."

"Nah, that's just Ian's name for it." He examined a beat-up old bicycle that leaned against François's house. "I bet that bike rides about the way François walks." He did an imitation.

"It's not nice to laugh at people's infirmities."

"You've gotten very superior, I must say. That school you go to must be a real snob job."

"It's a very good school." I walked ahead of him along the path past the other slave houses. We inspected them all. Mostly they were empty except for dirt, and here and there an old whiskey bottle and some broken Coke bottles. Franklin found a rusty knife. The houses smelled of mildew, like the big house, only worse. In the last one, I jumped backward and nearly knocked Franklin over. There was a snake coiled in the middle of the dirt floor. Franklin wanted to kill it, but I wouldn't let him. I was afraid it would turn out to be a cottonmouth or something and would kill him dead. I don't like snakes.

We passed an overturned wheelbarrow and a hoe, and a dug-up place where apparently François had made an attempt to weed a tangled rose garden. There was a kitchen garden with a high brick wall around it, where beans and lettuce and tomatoes were trying to grow, but they had to fight the weeds.

[31]

"It's a shame to let a place go like this," Franklin said. He swiped a couple of ripe tomatoes for us.

It was steaming hot again, but although I was nervous about snakes and spiders, the place was interesting. Everything grew wild now, all tangled up, but you could see a field where some crop had been grown. Franklin thought it was sugarcane. "They all grew sugarcane." As we got deeper into the woods, there were lots of camphor trees and willows and palmettos, tulip trees, camellia bushes; and everywhere there were thick vines like ropes, that seemed to trip you and grab at you as if they were alive. Toadstools were enormous. You could see traces of a brick walk, but the bricks were moldy and covered with moss, and pretty soon they gave out altogether, and the woods got too thick to walk in.

Coming back we took a different path, one that led toward the river. We stopped at a pond where a flock of wild geese took off.

Once we stopped breathless and still at a noise far behind us that sounded like a woman's scream.

"What was that?" I clutched my brother's arm.

We listened hard, but there was no other sound except the insects and birds. "Probably some nutty bird like our New Hampshire loon."

"Loons only scream at night."

"So Louisiana loons are loony. Come on."

The land was flat, but the thick brush and weeds

all tangled up made it hard to walk. I kept tripping. Once a big plant with leaves like daggers stabbed me and made my arm bleed.

"Even the plants attack us." I felt as if we were in some strange land a million miles from other human beings. It was one of those days when you want to sob like a five-year-old and yell, "Mama, I want to go home."

Huge spider webs hit me in the face, swinging down from the trees. Then all of a sudden we were at the river. Down here it was wide and muddy and irregular, full of inlets and weird little islands of long rushes and twisty mangrove trees.

"Watch it," Franklin said. "You could get sucked up in this swampy stuff."

"I sure wouldn't want to get lost out there in a boat."

"That's why the pirates liked it. They knew every inch of it, and they could hide out. I wonder if we're near the Bayou Barataria."

"What's that?"

"One of Lafitte's hangouts. They say he's buried there, but it's doubtful." Franklin had read every book ever written about Jean Lafitte. He shied a pebble at a lizard. "Maybe El Creepo would drive me down there."

"Don't call Ian names. He's nice."

"I know. But why does he laugh like that?"

[33]

"People can't help how they laugh."

He was walking ahead of me, and he stopped short. I had to step around him to see what he was looking at. Right in front of us, almost hidden by trees, was a cabin. In front of the cabin a black boy, about sixteen or seventeen years old, was sitting on the ground fooling with a fishing pole. Behind him on the doorsill of the cabin sat a very old black man who seemed to be dozing.

At that moment the boy looked up and saw us. You could see him stiffen, but he got up in a leisurely way and waited.

Franklin walked toward him, and I followed. "Hi," Franklin said.

The boy said, "Hi."

"We were just out for a walk." Franklin said. "We didn't know this cabin was here. Didn't mean to barge onto your property."

"That's okay."

The two boys studied each other for a minute, and then the black boy said, "You care to set down?" Without waiting for an answer he got a couple of wooden stools that were leaning against the house. We sat down.

"We're from Belle Rêve." I said.

"Temporarily," Franklin said. "Very temporarily."

For the first time the boy smiled. He had a nice

smile. In fact he was very good-looking.

The old man awoke with a start and said, "Eh?"

"Grandpère," the boy said, "these folks are from Belle Rêve."

"Just visiting," Franklin said. "Renting, actually." **2103765**

He seemed to be making a great point of our not being permanent. Maybe because everyone at Belle Rêve seemed a little crazy.

The old man rubbed his eyes, stood up, and shook hands with us. "*Bon jour*," he said. "Welcome. Justin, bring somet'ing. Some pecans."

Justin went into the cabin and came back with a box like the ones they pack strawberries in and passed it around. They were pecans, but they were sugar-coated and wonderful. I said so, and Justin said, "We still got a little sugarcane under cultivation. In the fall when you separate the molasses from the sugar, you dip the pecans into the sugar."

"They're terrific." Franklin took a couple more.

The old man chuckled, pointed a bent finger at Franklin, and said to the boy, "*Bon parti.*"

"What does that mean?" Franklin said.

"He says you're a good boy, fine boy."

I was feeling left out. I said, "Could you tell me what that plant is that has a lot of sharp spikes going out in all directions?" My arm still smarted.

"How tall?"

[*35*]

"Oh, taller than I am. With blossoms on top, kind of closed up."

"That's Spanish dagger. The blossoms open at night."

"Oh. Thank you." I couldn't think of anything else to say.

The old man said something in French, and Justin said to us, "He wants to know, have you seen old François?"

"Yes," Franklin said.

"He wants to know, was he drunk?"

"Kind of."

Justin spoke to the old man in French, and the old man growled something. Justin laughed. "My grandpère, he hates old François. François steals his fruit, and sometimes his tools."

"You don't talk with a French accent like everybody else," Franklin said.

The boy shrugged. "I went to American school in Baton Rouge. My father was an American."

"Aren't these other people American?" I was surprised.

"Sure, but, you know, we say French are French, American are American. Sure, I guess we're all American now."

"Do your parents live here, too?" Franklin said.

"No. My father is dead. My mother got married again."

Franklin's eyebrows shot up. "Did it upset you?"

"Why upset? She had the little kids to bring up. He's a good man that she married. Why upset?"

"Oh, I don't know. No reason. I guess. Sometimes it's hard to get used to." Franklin walked away and looked at a chopping block. He touched the axe handle.

"Do you live here all the time?" I asked Justin.

"I do now. I like it here. And—" he ducked his head toward his grandfather "—he's getting old. He needs somebody. You want to see the house?"

I thought he meant the cabin, but he took us down a path and there was this really pretty house, not nearly as big as Belle Rêve, but the same kind of well-proportioned Greek-looking house with two story pillars and an upper gallery. It didn't have the two wings that Belle Rêve had, and the roof was a lot steeper, with a fenced-in place on top of the roof. I asked what it was for.

"It's a belvedere," Justin said. "The owner used to watch the river from there."

"Was he a pirate?" Franklin asked hopefully.

Justin laughed. "Nah. He raised cane, like everybody else. When he died, his family was all gone, and he left the place to the people that had worked for him a long time. They've all died or moved away now except my grandfather."

The paint on the house was peeling in some

places, and the steps were broken, but it looked in pretty good repair otherwise.

"We try to keep it up," Justin said, "but it takes a lot of work, that and the garden, too."

"Do you live off the place?" Franklin asked.

"Yeah, pretty much. We grow vegetables, and I fish a lot. We make out all right."

He took us through the house. A lot of the furniture was still there, with dust covers on it. Justin knocked down a spider web. "Hard to keep up with it all. Down here the country takes over faster'n you can hold it back." He straightened an oil painting of a stout man in a black suit. "That was Michie Le-Blanc. 'Michie,' that was the black man's word for '*monsieur.*'"

When we walked back, Justin's grandfather was chopping wood, and he didn't look so old any more. His short arms moved up and down in a steady rhythm. When he saw us, he stopped, smiled, and said, "Wait a moment, *s'il vous plait.*" He went into the cabin and came back carrying two oranges, the nice greenish kind that are tree-ripened and not colored artificially. He gave one to Justin and one to me.

"*Pour la petite jolie,*" he said.

I know enough French to know when somebody calls me pretty. I was really pleased. We thanked him and said goodbye.

[*38*]

"Come over if you want to go fishing," Justin said to Franklin. Then he smiled at me. "You too."

"Have you got a pirogue?" Franklin asked.

"Nah. Pirogues tip over too easy. I got a good old flat-bottomed bateau."

On the way home, Franklin said, "Those are the first friendly people we've met."

"They were really nice." I began to peel my orange.

"Don't litter," Franklin said, and we both laughed. The ground where we were walking was so swampy, you could drop a piece of orange peel and it would be out of sight in seconds.

We were nearly home when we saw an old woman picking wild flowers. She was off in a little clearing away from the path, and we almost didn't see her at all.

"Who's that?" Franklin said.

"Who knows." We stopped to look. She was wearing a long purple skirt, a kind of shawl, and a bonnet like the ones ladies wore when they went West on covered wagons.

She looked up and saw us, and at once hunched up her shoulders, raised her arms with her hands hanging limp, so that she looked like some giant bat, and began to shriek in a high cracked voice: "Cut-cut-cut-cut," like an angry hen.

[*39*]

We got out of there.

"Jeez," Franklin said. "You don't think Belle Rêve is an insane asylum, do you?"

"She may not belong to Belle Rêve. There are other places around. The village isn't actually far away, remember? We drove through it."

"Well, wherever she's from, she gives me the creeps. They all give me the creeps. Let's ask Mother if we can go back to Grandma's."

Franklin went straight upstairs when we got home, but I went looking for Mother. She was with Ian in the dining room. She had propped one of her watercolors up against the hurricane lamp, and they were looking at it, back to me. He had his arm around her, and after a minute she reached up and kissed him. It made me feel both sad and happy.

Ian turned his head and saw me, and his face turned bright red. I muttered, "Excuse me," and fled. I hadn't meant to spy on them.

He wasn't there at dinner, and Mom seemed depressed. When we were alone, I said, "Look, I didn't mean to embarrass Ian. I didn't know you were there . . ."

"Oh, I know." She sounded discouraged. "He thinks you resent him."

"But I don't. And you know how Franklin is; it takes him forever to make friends."

"I know, I've tried to explain." She sighed. "Human relationships are so complicated."

Franklin had been bugging me to ask her if we could leave early for Grandma's, but I didn't have the heart to do it now. "Mama," I said, "don't be depressed. We're really glad you married again. You won't feel so lonely now."

She cheered up a little. "I'm lucky to have such nice children."

"Well, *we're* lucky to have you."

She smiled. "I'll keep it in mind. We're a family of lucky ducks."

That sounded more like our Mom, and I felt better.

4

I SLEPT LATE the next morning. During the night I had lain awake a long time thinking about Mom. Was depression habit-forming? I got so hungry that after I heard the others go to bed, I went downstairs and made a sandwich. On the way back I stopped to look at that painting. It was really eerie-looking in the shadows cast by the night-light at the head of the stairs. I thought I saw a resemblance to Eva, and I wondered if it were her mother. I went back to bed and tried to figure out if the dates were right. It was hard to tell how old Eva was, but probably she could have had a mother whose debut was in 1916. Something about Jasmine's eyes looked kind of like Eva's eyes, although Jasmine looked fierce and Eva looked scared. They both looked more than a little mad.

I was still thinking about it when I heard a peculiar sound. It was familiar but so out of place, I couldn't identify it at first. But that was what it was, all right—a power lawn mower. In the pitch dark? At one o'clock in the morning?

I got up and looked between the slats of the jalousies. Outside, a dark blob was moving around on the stretch of lawn in front of the house. I'd noticed when we came that it hadn't been mowed for a long time. Braving mosquitoes I opened the window to see better. Somebody was mowing the lawn. Not in the usual way, but in great circles and jagged sweeps. And that somebody was singing. It had to be old François, drunk as a skunk, again.

I heard people moving around the house, probably Ian or Mother or both, but I didn't join them. I just watched. After a minute somebody shouted from the wing. I recognized Felicité's raspy voice. As far as I knew, she was the only one around. Eva's car hadn't come back from New Orleans.

The lawn mower made such a sharp turn, it almost tipped over, and then it headed for the wing. It went right across a flowerbed and out of my line of vision. But I heard a crash and a screech of rage. He must have hit the corner of the house. Then there was a real bedlam of yells and curses, and you couldn't sort out the voices any more. Until there was one long woman's scream. Then silence. I waited a little while, but nothing more happened, as far as I could tell. It had been enough, though, to make me sure we had put ourselves into a nest of lunatics.

THE SUNLIGHT was filtering through the jalousies, making wavy patterns on the floor. It was Saturday morning, and what had waked me up was Eva. She knocked and then walked right in, carrying a stack of sheets that came to her chin. Behind her in the hall I could see a strange man. I let out a small yelp.

"Eva, watch it," the man in the hall said, "the girl is still in bed."

"Oh, I'm sorry," Eva said, coming right in. "I won't be a minute. The linens are kept in here . . ." She had gone to a big wardrobe affair with shelves that stood in one corner of the room. "The laundry came back, and I have to take inventory. I won't be long." She didn't seem shy now. In fact, she seemed almost unaware of my being there.

"Can't you do it later?" the man said. He was tactfully facing away from the door.

"Arthur, I can't. The inventory has to be taken." She began putting sheets on the shelves and calling them out to him. "Arthur, here are the two blue sheets, doubles, one contour, one not. Have you checked that?"

"Check," he said.

"Two pink striped sheets, double, both flat. Got it?"

"Got it."

This went on for about five minutes. Then she said, "Oh, dear."

"Now what?" he said.

"One set of single whites are missing. Felicité was right."

"Probably Felicité stole them," he said.

I couldn't help giggling. I heard him laugh. Was it possible there was a normal person here? I tried to get a look at him. He was shorter than Eva, who was tall and bony, like a horse. He had curly hair, worn longish, and he was wearing a teal blue short-sleeved polo shirt, the kind that usually has an alligator on the front, although I couldn't see that. And he wore white shorts and Adidas. I wished I could see his face, but I appreciated his decency about not standing there staring at me.

"Let me count them all once more to make sure."

"Eva, you're obsessed," he said.

"Arthur," she said in a whiny voice, "you don't understand. I have to be efficient about this."

"You are missing one pair of white sheets. It is so noted. Now will you please come along and let that poor girl get up or go back to sleep or whatever she wants."

Eva gave me a startled glance, as if she had just

remembered me. "Oh, yes, of course. Sorry." And she was gone, closing the door with a slight bang.

I got up and dressed, wondering who Arthur could be. I hoped he was not her boyfriend. If he was, God help him. Though he did seem younger than Eva.

I found Franklin waiting for me with considerable impatience. Neither Mother nor Ian was around.

"Do you have to sleep all day?" he said.

I explained what had happened, and after I had some cold corn bread and milk, we went outside. It was cloudy and hotter than ever. The air was like a wet blanket.

"Did you hear the racket last night?" my brother asked.

"Who could miss it. What happened in the end, do you know?"

"Old François took off a piece of the house. Why didn't you come out to look?"

"I upset Ian. So I didn't want to take a chance on seeing him again." I told him what had happened.

"I upset Mom," Franklin said gloomily. "I asked her if we could leave, and she burst into tears." He sighed. "We could write Grandma to send us air fare."

"No, we've got to stay here and make Ian believe we like him. To cheer up Mom."

We came around the corner of the house and

saw where the mower had hit. It was still there, on its side, and there was a gouge out of the siding on the house.

"That's one corner Ian won't want a picture of," I said.

"Incidentally Mom said we were to stay away from the slave quarters."

"Why?"

"She says François might get rough."

"Baloney."

"That's what I said. I think something odd is going on around here, and she wants us to keep out of it." He smiled. "But what's the point of being here if we don't rush in where angels fear to tread?"

That was a family joke, that line; it was what Dad used to say about us.

At the junction of the paths I said, "Shall we go on, or shall we go fishing with Justin?"

"Let's see first if old François got back on his feet. I wonder if he hurt himself when the mower rammed the house."

"Alcoholics and babies don't get hurt."

We sauntered down the shabby brick path and casually approached François's place. The door was wide open, and the room seemed empty. To be sure, Franklin put his head in the door and said, "Morning." No answer.

All the slave quarters were empty. Locusts were

making a racket, and enormous grasshoppers leaped away from our feet. It must have been about ninety-nine percent humidity. A lizard clung to the wall of the last house and disappeared even while I was looking at him. I kept an eye out for snakes, as we started down a narrow path.

"Do you really think something funny is going on? It's not just me and my imagination?"

"I think everybody around here is crazy, the whole lot of them on this place, and anything could happen."

As he finished speaking, there was a commotion in the bushes. The branches were so thick, you couldn't see what it was, but someone or something went crashing off.

When we got up enough nerve to look, we could see how the ground was trampled. "An animal," I said. "Dog, maybe."

Franklin held up a scrap of torn cloth. "Wearing a purple dress?"

"We'd better get off this path," I said, trying not to let my voice shake. "Come on. This place is getting too strange."

I turned, trying to look casual as I twisted my hair into a knot and tied it up in the back with my scarf. If I lived in this climate, I'd get a butch. We walked back toward the house, but between the heat and the questions in my mind, it was hard to push my feet out ahead of me. I had to fight myself not to keep looking over my shoulder.

Franklin stopped finally, just outside the potting shed, and pointed at an old rubber boot that lay on the ground. "Funny place to leave a boot."

"I said, "I guess in this climate if you take something off, you let it stay where it falls."

We heard Eva's car start up and in a minute saw it drive off with two people in it. Eva and Arthur.

"Mom doesn't know who he is," Franklin said. "I think she figures he might be a boyfriend."

"Do witches have boyfriends?"

"Sure. Warlocks." He pushed open the door of the potting shed to put the rubber boot inside, but dropped it instead. He stepped back so fast, I thought he'd seen a snake.

"What's the matter?"

"Look," he said.

Old François lay on the floor all crumpled up, one of his boots off. The shed reeked of whiskey and other smells, like pesticides. A nearly empty pint of whiskey was upright beside him, and just behind him a shovel and a hoe and some other garden tools were strewn around. He had a nasty gash on his forehead, and his face was gray.

"He must be sleeping it off," Franklin said uneasily.

"There's blood on the floor."

"He must have cut himself when he fell off the mower. Somebody ought to do something about him. An old man like that, he could . . . he could die."

"We'd better find Mom."

"They went on a tour of plantation houses."

"And Eva's gone. We'll have to tell Felicité."

Relieved to think of a way to dump the responsibility, we ran to the house and banged on the kitchen door in Eva's wing.

Felicité came to the door, wiping her hands on her apron and scowling at being interrupted. She'd been peeling onions, and her eyes were red.

"So?" She glared at us.

"We thought," Franklin said, "we thought somebody ought to know that François is lying on the floor in the potting shed . . ."

She looked blank. "In da what?"

"Where the garden tools and flowerpots are," I said. "He's cut his head. He looks real sick."

She looked past us toward the outbuildings, as if considering what we had said. "He dronk," she said with a shrug. "Sleepin' it off."

"But he has this bad cut on his head," Franklin said. "His face is gray."

"Eh? Gray? What is gray?"

"His face," I said. "He looks sick. He almost looks—" I was going to say "dead," but she interrupted me.

"Okay, okay, I go fix heem up. I take him coffee."

"You'd better take a bandage or something . . ."

She waved her arms at us, "Okay, okay, I say I go fix heem up. Me, I don' have da time, but I do it." She shut the door in our faces.

"Well," Franklin muttered, "you're welcome."

We went down to Justin's place, but nobody was around, so we sat on their little broken-down wharf and watched the Mississippi go by.

That night at dinner Mother and Ian were both in a really good mood. Mother told us all about the plantation they'd been to see, a place called Oak Alley. "It's real name is Bon Sèjour," she said, "but everybody calls it Oak Alley because there's a fabulous drive. Twenty-eight enormous oaks, with trunks about twenty feet around. The trees are ninety feet apart from each other, but they're so big, their branches overlap. It's incredibly beautiful. And the house at the end of the alley, restored and lived in, a lovely, lovely pink house—"

Ian interrupted. "With the most beautiful fan transom I've ever seen. Ironwork made years ago by the slaves. Oh, it's a wonder. Worth the trip."

They kept on talking about Oak Alley all through dinner. Finally right at the end, Mother said, "And what have you two been up to?"

"We found a body in the potting shed," Franklin said, with a bored shrug.

Mother and Ian exchanged amused looks.

"Really?" Ian said. "Who was this person in the potting shed?"

"Oh, only old François."

Mother looked startled. "What do you mean?"

"Oh, he's kidding," I said. "Sort of. François had passed out. And he had a bad cut on his head."

"Last night's adventure, I expect," Ian said. "That sounded like a bit of a smash, there at the end." He put down his napkin and got up.

"Eva isn't here," Mother said. "Should we check?"

"Oh, I'll pop down there and take a look. I daresay he's ambulatory by now, though possibly off on another binge. The old boy does rather soak it up, doesn't he."

"I wonder why Eva keeps him on," Mother said.

"Maybe she holds him in thrall," I said.

"I told you children not to hang around François." She looked concerned.

"Well, he's safe when he's unconscious." Franklin said.

"Please." "I don't want anything happening to spoil our time together."

Later Ian came back and said, "Nobody in sight. I checked the potting shed and François's digs, but no sign of him. He's probably gone into the village for a new bottle." He gave us a grin that was meant to reassure us.

"There's a pint in the potting shed, with some whiskey in it," I said.

"Didn't see any. The potting shed looked quite spic and span, in fact. Looks as if Felicité must have taken a mop to it."

We went upstairs and Franklin and I sat out on my gallery. "Funny about that bottle," I said.

"Why? Felicité no doubt heaved it into the trash."

"I think I'll have a look," I said.

"Why? What's on your mind?"

"I don't really know. Something bothers me."

"This whole place bothers me. But I might as well come with you. There's nothing else to do."

We went down the back stairs and out through the kitchen to the little enclosure where the trash cans were kept. Looking through garbage is not my ideal pastime, but it didn't take long to determine that there weren't any whiskey bottles there. We beat off the greenheads and departed from that smelly enclosure.

"Let's ask Felicité if François is all right," I said.

"She'll knock our heads off."

"So what. I don't think she'll really kill us."

"Don't be too sure! Why are you so curious, anyway?"

[53]

"You don't have to come." I went to the kitchen door in the wing and knocked. A light was on, near the door, but no one came.

"She isn't going to bother answering."

The door wasn't shut quite tight. I pushed it open a little and looked in. Someone was sitting at the far end of the room, deep in shadows, rocking slowly in a rocking chair, her back toward me. I didn't think it was Felicité,—it looked too tall. Maybe Eva was back. I said, "Felicité?"

Whoever it was in the chair got up and went through the other door so fast her chair went on rocking.

"Well?" Franklin had stayed away from the door. "Was she there?"

"No, but someone else was."

"Who?"

"I don't know. It was too dark to see. A woman. She whipped out of there as if I'd scared her to death."

"You shouldn't step into people's houses. Mom would be mad."

I didn't answer him because I was trying to wade through all the things that had happened, trying to find some clue to the relationships between all these people. Something, I felt, was not right, but I didn't know what. I said I was going to bed and read, but what I really did was go to bed and think.

It was really none of my business, the problems of this house. Yet I was there and had nothing else to do. It would give my imagination a workout.

I couldn't sleep. The trouble with thinking I discovered was that I didn't know what it was I wanted to think about. I only knew that something about François bothered me. I wished we had checked to see if he were breathing. I kept having this feeling that when we saw him, he was dead. I considered talking to Mom about it, but she was sitting downstairs with Ian, and I knew what kind of reaction I'd get if I wandered in and said, "Hey, Mom, I think maybe old François was dead." There'd be that look between them, and then Mom would be half amused, half annoyed because she had told us to stay away from François. There'd be talk about my vivid imagination, et cetera et cetera. And I'd go back to bed with nothing changed, feeling like a fool.

Eventually I heard them come up to their bedroom. I listened to their quiet voices and then the sound of a bath running and pretty soon their bedroom door closing.

From my room I couldn't actually see the lights in Eva's wing, but usually I could catch a glow outside the windows. It seemed to be dark tonight. But eventually I heard something, a low noise from outside. I sat up in bed and listened hard. It was a sound

[55]

I knew but couldn't quite place at first. Then I had it. It was the squeak and thud of old François's wheelbarrow. So he was all right after all, and I had just been imagining things.

I flopped back on my pillow. Just as I was falling asleep, I heard Eva's car come in and saw the lights reflected from the wing. Then I slept.

5

"WHAT WAS THE COMMOTION in the wing last night?"
Franklin said after breakfast.

"What commotion?"

"Real late. It woke me up. A car came in . . ."

"That was Eva. I went to sleep after that."

"Well, there was something going on in the
wing. All the lights went on, and I could hear loud
voices, and after a long time another car came, and
pretty soon went away again."

I yawned. "I don't know. I think those people
are the kind that are always in a stew. Anyway,
François is all right."

"How do you know?"

I told him about the wheelbarrow.

He laughed. "That's a relief. Crazy old François.
Gardening by the light of the moon. Maybe he's

part troll." He squinted his eyes at me. "You thought the old guy was dead or something, didn't you?"

"Oh, not necessarily. I just thought he looked very odd."

"If I'd thought he might be dead, I'd have checked his pulse."

I laughed. "You wouldn't have touched him with a ten-foot pole."

"Oh, yeah?" He changed the subject. "This is Sunday."

"So?"

"So where are the Sunday papers? I want to read the comics."

"There's a box for papers out at the gate. Two boxes, in fact. One says HOUSE, one says WING. Maybe they leave them there."

"Let's go look."

We walked down the weed-streaked walk to the gate, and sure enough, there was a Sunday paper and also yesterday's paper in the HOUSE box. I peered into the other box; there was mail there as well. Obviously they weren't any better than we were about picking it up.

"You are the nosiest kid in the universe," Franklin said. "Don't touch that. It's a misdemeanor punishable by enormous fines and years in prison to touch the U.S. mail."

"Who's touching?" It wasn't interesting anyway. A bill from Sears, an advertising circular from Bombay Furniture, an electric light bill. We went back to the front porch and read the comics.

We didn't see anyone in the wing, although you could tell there were people in there. Eva's car was in the yard, and now and then you could hear sounds, like silver dumped into a dishpan, or the jalousies being shut on one of the long windows, and once a loud voice and then silence.

In the afternoon Eva came out alone and drove off. It was a hot, sleepy day, with thunderclouds piling up over the river. We spoke of going to see Justin, but we were too lazy to do it. Maybe tomorrow, we said. Ian made something called Ramos Gin Fizzes, which tasted like ice cream sodas but had real gin. We only got to sip a little of Mom's, and then she made us some lemonade. Ian spent all afternoon making a gumbo for dinner. One thing you had to say for him, he could cook.

During dinner the wind began to blow.

"It's too early for hurricanes, isn't it?" Mother said, and Ian said he didn't know if they were ever actually out of season.

Shutters were banging and the wind was screaming down the chimneys, and then the rain came, driving and hard. We all ran around the house closing

[59]

windows; but some of those old ones wouldn't stay latched; as soon as you closed them, they would pull loose and clatter and bang like mad. It didn't seem as if the wind could blow any harder, but it did. Tree branches lashed the windows, and vines pulled loose and hung limp and wet. When you looked out, everything seemed to be bending to the wind. Ian ran out to make sure the windows were shut on the station wagon, and we had literally to pull him back in the kitchen door. He was soaked, and his hair was plastered to his head as if he'd been in the shower.

We could hardly talk to each other, the wind was so noisy. And after we finally went to bed, the storm kept me awake. Lightning would flash every once in a while, and then there would be a clap of thunder that sounded as if it were right inside my skull. The colors outside looked strange, everything kind of underwater green. And then it got too black to see anything. I put on my light and reread the comics and read the editorial page and the want ads and some real estate offerings, until I thought boredom would put me to sleep. But when I dropped the paper to the floor and put out the light, I was still too revved up to sleep.

The thunder and lightning seemed to be moving away from us, but the wind and the rain kept up their attack. I wondered what it would be like in a hurricane. Maybe not so different from this.

Much later I thought I heard someone. I decided it must be Franklin prowling around, though he's usually a sound sleeper, so I got up and opened my door. I've never fainted, but I came close right then. A woman, her back toward me, was standing in front of the portrait of Jasmine, a knife in her hand. She wore a long purple skirt and a red velvet cape slung around her shoulders. Water from her clothes dripped on the floor.

I guess I shrieked because she whirled toward me. For a moment she stood still, the knife held up, and I was sure she was going to come at me; but instead she turned and ran for the stairs, skittering along like an animal. As she went downstairs a flash of lightning lit her up for a moment, and I saw that it was the woman who'd been picking flowers in the woods. It was no stranger then, but someone who belonged.

I ran after her, feeling for some reason less afraid. But by the time I got to the landing, she had fled out the front door, leaving it wide open to the rain. I struggled to close it, with rain and wind beating at me. And only when I got it closed and leaned against it, did I fully realize what had happened. Suddenly I was too weak to move.

When I came back upstairs I looked at the painting. I couldn't see it very well in the dark so I turned on the hall light. There was a slash mark across the words "Jasmine on her debut." What did Jasmine have to do with everything else? I needed help.

At my mother's bedroom door I stopped. Scared though I was, I couldn't bring myself to knock. I did knock on Franklin's door and went in to try and wake him, but you might as well try to wake the dead.

There was nothing else to do then but to go back to my room and brace a chair under the door-knob and pull the covers up to my chin.

6

I TOLD THEM at breakfast what had happened. Franklin gave a little gasp, and my mother and Ian exchanged glances. I saw at once that they weren't going to believe me.

"You must have been dreaming, dear," my mother said.

"Mother, I was not dreaming."

"Then why didn't the rest of us hear this person?"

"This person," indeed. She was beginning to sound as English as Ian. "She was right outside my door."

"So that's who the flower lady was," Franklin said. "Jasmine."

"Of course," my mother said, as if it were common knowledge. "I painted her one day, or started to till she saw me and fled. I saw the resemblance right away. But truly, Dorothy, I think you had that portrait on your mind and you dreamed you saw her."

"Mother, the floor by the front door is still wet."

"The door must have blown open."

"It was *pushed* open. I closed it." I was furious. There is nothing more frustrating than not being believed.

"In any case," Ian said, apparently thinking he was making peace, "it's of no great consequence, is it. I mean no harm done."

"Except for the slash on the painting." I hadn't mentioned that when I told the story. I had the satisfaction of seeing my mother look up with a new expression.

"What slash?"

"If you'd care to come with me, I'll show you." I led them upstairs and pointed out the cut on the painting. No one said a word.

Finally Ian gave a little laugh and said, "I say, you wouldn't have done it yourself as a sort of joke on us, would you?"

That did it. I turned on him and said, "I am not into that type of joke, and although you may not believe it, I am entirely sane." I stalked into my room and slammed the door.

Pretty soon there was a knock, and Mother came in. "Dorothy," she said, "I am not pleased with the way you behaved just now."

"I don't know what you expect of us."

"I expect common courtesy, to begin with. Ian's feelings are hurt. You were quite rude."

I felt guilty. "Mother, you don't know how hard we try. But we loved Dad, and it isn't always easy to adjust to someone new. We do like Ian. We *are* glad you're happy. But he seems to see us as a pair of unreliable children."

"I know it isn't easy." She sounded tired. "It's partly Ian's own fault—he's so sure you won't like him. And he's not used to young people, except as students." She patted my hand. "I'm sure you didn't mean to hurt him. We'll just all keep on trying." But she looked sad, and I felt like a heel.

Later in the day Ian and Franklin went into the city to buy groceries, and Mom went around to the far side of the empty wing to work on a painting. I was still worried about upsetting her, so I followed her and asked if she'd mind if I watched.

She shook her head. At the moment she was peering in through the dirt-streaked windows of the wing. "What a pity they've let it all go. Look at that marvelous fireplace. And I'll bet there are beautiful antiques under those sheets."

"Not like the Salvation Army stuff in our part of the house."

"Well, we're only renters." She gave a little squeal of delight. "Dorothy, look! A rocking horse."

It was hard to see anything through all the dirt and cobwebs on the windows, but I finally saw it— a handsome wooden rocking horse standing in a corner.

"Oh, I wish I could paint it for Ian. He was telling me the other day about a rocking horse he adored as a child." She got her sketch pad and came back to the window, but after a few minutes, she gave up in impatience. "I can't see it well enough." She sounded depressed, and I realized that little things still threw her into a spin.

"Don't worry. The one you're doing of the house is great."

She worked a little while, frowning. "I hope Franklin is not sitting in stony silence while Ian makes frantic efforts to get a conversation going."

"Franklin is a man of two words," I said, " 'yes' and 'no.' "

She laughed, but she didn't look happy. Finally she threw down her brush and said, "My head aches."

"Come in and lie down, Mom. It's too hot out here."

I made her some lemonade, and got her to lie down with a cold cloth on her face. And it was then that I had my idea about the rocking horse. In my suitcase I had the Polaroid camera that Aunt Maggie had given me for Christmas, which I always forgot to use till too late. With a little luck I could pry open a window of the empty wing and get a picture of the rocking horse that Mom could work from.

When I got outside, the sky had clouded up, and it looked as dark as evening. I thought about Franklin and hoped he was having a good time. He hadn't wanted to go.

I moved hastily around to the wing and decided just for the heck of it to try the door. Our door was never locked; maybe this one wasn't either. At first it seemed to be, but when I pushed hard, it flew open so suddenly I almost fell into the room.

The moment I was in, I was kind of sorry I was there. With all the jalousies closed, it was dark, and the white-draped furniture looked really spooky. For a minute I couldn't even find the darned rocking horse, and then I wasn't sure my camera would work right in that dim light. I know from nothing about cameras, but Aunt Maggie had said this one was foolproof. Well, this would be the ultimate test.

[67]

I took three shots from different angles, and then decided on one more. I was so intent on what I was doing that I stumbled over a low table and nearly fell flat on my face.

It was then, as I was struggling to get my balance, that something came down over my head and shut out all light. I felt as if I were pinioned inside some heavy cloth thing. When I tried to scream, I couldn't make a sound. It was suffocating under the cloth. I flopped around the room, trying to get my arms free, trying to get out of that awful room, but at first all I could do was crash into furniture, bang my shins, hit my head against walls.

After what seemed like a hundred and fifty years, I got my arms free and ran for the door. The shroudlike thing still clung to me, and when I got outside, I saw it was one of those big cloth sugar bags, all dirty and mildewed. I thought I was going to have hysterics right then and there. No bag like that could have gotten over my head by itself. Someone had put it there. To calm down, I went back to the house and took a bath and washed my hair.

I lay in that tub of hot water a long time, trying to stop shaking and wanting to vomit. I couldn't get the smell of mildew out of my nose. But my main problem was that I was scared. A dropcloth could have fallen on me and covered me. That I could have understood. But a sugar bag could not have fallen on me open in such a way that I wound up inside—not without help. Someone had done it. But who, and why? And why hadn't I heard anyone? I puzzled in fear and anger, longing to tell someone, not sure anyone, even Franklin, would believe me.

The funny thing was that I had hung onto my camera all through that ordeal, and when I looked I had two excellent and one fair picture of the rocking horse. Before dinner I gave them to my mother, with no word of what I had gone through to get them. It was almost worth it (but not quite) when I saw how her face lit up. She told me not to go in there again though. "It's not our house."

"Don't worry," I said.

That night at dinner Ian said, "I had a chat with good old Félicité, by the way, and she says it may indeed have been Eva's mother wandering in here. The old girl gets mixed up in her head. She lives in a rest home, but she comes home to visit."

Just as I was thinking, So that's who it was, he said, "Eva took her back to the rest home early this morning. Perfectly natural when you think of it, for an old girl to get confused like that. She did use to live in this house after all. Oh, and in case you're curious, old François has gone to visit his sister. All should be quiet on the western front from now on."

After dinner Franklin disappeared, and when I

went to find him, he was down by the garçonnière looking puzzled.

"Now what?" I said.

"The strangest thing. Come and look."

I followed him inside. In a corner, neatly out of the way, was one muddy rubber boot, a hoe, and a pint whiskey bottle partly full, a lot of nails, screws, paintbrushes stiff with dried paint, a torn dropcloth and some tools.

"Those things were not here before," he said.

"Why is it so strange? We know Felicité cleaned up the potting shed."

"But why put this stuff in here? Wouldn't the natural thing be to heave the bottle in the trash and put the boot in François's house? It's his boot, after all. And the hoe. Why move the hoe? And all that other stuff, that belongs in the potting shed."

I went closer. "That hoe has a dark stain on it."

"Like mud?"

"Or like blood." I picked up the bottle and sniffed it. "Franklin, this isn't whiskey."

"So what is it?"

"Weed killer or something like that. Smell it." I held it out, and he sniffed and made a face.

"François shouldn't put weed killer in a whiskey bottle. It would be easy to make a mistake and drink it, especially if you were half smashed."

"Maybe we should dump it out or throw it in the trash."

"No, leave it there."

"Why?"

He shrugged. "You never know."

"Never know what?"

"You just never know."

On the way back home, I told him about my adventure in the wing. As I had suspected might be the case, he was not completely convinced someone else had been there. "This whole place is such a mess," he said, "anything can fall from anywhere." I did not argue. And we soon both went to bed. That night, to my surprise, I slept.

The next morning we decided to go to see Justin. He was home this time, but not in the mood for fishing, as we had hoped he might be. "Man, I been out fishing for two days. Grandpère and me, we went out on my uncle Gaston's shrimp boat. I don't want to see another fish for a while. Shrimp stink, I'm telling you."

His grandfather was sawing up an old tree that had fallen down in the storm. I noticed again how strong he was for a man his age.

"Well, old François won't bother your grandfather for a while," Franklin said.

"How come?"

"He's gone to visit his sister."

Justin widened his eyes. Then he called to his grandfather in French. He said something about François, and the old man looked at him in a puzzled way, and then answered in French.

"What's he say?" Franklin asked.

"Said old François ain't got any family around here. Old François came here way back, years and years back when he was a young man. He was a Cajun, came here from Lafayette."

"Did he ever get married?" I asked.

Justin asked his grandfather, who put down his saw and came over to us. He pushed his boating cap onto the back of his head and scratched his curly gray hair. Justin asked him again, "Did old François ever marry?"

The old man chuckled and shook his head. In English he said, "They don' 'low that."

We were puzzled.

"Who don't 'low what, Grandpère?" Justin said.

But he only laughed again and said, "Masta', he run him off."

We were consumed with curiosity, but we couldn't get him to say any more. Pretty soon he went into the cabin and didn't come out again. And after a while we went home.

As if we had discussed it, we walked right past

the house and kept on going down by the slave quarters, toward the old cane field and the swampy
woods. Neither of us said much.

Finally I said, "What are we thinking about
anyway?"

Franklin gave me a wary look. "I dunno. What
are *you* thinking about?"

"I don't know." Again we walked in silence,
just strolling along. The ground was wet and mushy
after all that rain. I said, "If people do die, I mean if
they *do* die, what happens?"

Franklin shrugged. "The undertaker comes and
carts 'em away."

"Medical examiner first," I said.

"So medical examiner. What of it?"

"Well, I mean it isn't anything to make a big
secret of, is it?"

"Shouldn't think so."

Silence. Something Franklin just said was echo-
ing in my mind. "What did you say the undertaker
does?"

With a touch of impatience he said, "You know
what an undertaker does."

"Yes, but what was the word you used?"

He thought. "I said 'he carts 'em away.' "

"That's it." I stopped.

"What's what?"

"Cart. Remember I told you I heard something,

the night François . . . I mean the night after we had seen him sick?"

"So?"

"I thought it was his wheelbarrow."

"And?"

"Well, he couldn't have been pushing it around, could he, if he had a big cut in his head and a terrible hangover or whatever?"

"He might have." But Franklin was watching me. He was thinking what I was thinking. "But why?" he burst out. As often happened with us, he skipped the in-between questions, knowing I'd understand him.

"Exactly. Why would Felicité or whoever it was—"

"No one else was here."

"*She* was here."

"Jasmine. That's right. But I don't see Jasmine carting off an unconscious old man in a wheelbarrow—"

"She might. She hasn't got all her marbles, remember."

"Let's look for tracks."

The rain had washed away any tracks, if there had ever been any, but we kept on walking and looking. Suddenly Franklin grabbed my arm. "Look!" He pointed to a kind of ditch that lay between the dirt road and the far end of the deserted sugarcane field. There was a lot of mud and silt accumulated in the ditch, and there in plain view was the deep cut of one wheel. That was all. On the other side there was nothing. But Franklin had already jumped the ditch, careful not to disturb the track, and was moving like a hound trying to pick up a scent.

I wasn't too crazy about wading around in those tall weeds, but I followed him, pulling the bottoms of my jeans up high so I wouldn't accumulate a lot of weird bugs inside the legs.

Franklin stooped and picked something up, and I was almost afraid to look. But it was only an old four-handed saw, rusty and broken. He examined it carefully. "That's really old," he said. "I bet slaves used it, way back then."

"Tell Ian," I said.

Franklin went on through the high grass and flowers and tall stalks of what I suppose were the remains of cane. "The weeds have been broken," he said.

He was right. Something had been dragged through here. I began to feel very, very creepy, and if I hadn't been so curious, I'd have headed for home.

Finally, in front of us, we saw a small partly cleared place where somebody had once built a fire, or maybe lightning had scorched the ground. Franklin stopped again and pointed to the far side of this place. It looked recently dug up, and the earth was higher than the land around, sort of mounded up.

"Be careful," I said, but he was already walking toward it.

"Hey!" He yelled the word, and I jumped a foot. "Here's the wheelbarrow."

I caught up with him. Sure enough, there it was, lying on its side in tall weeds, almost hidden from sight. I was so excited, I took several steps toward it, forgetting all about weird bugs and such. Then Franklin said, "Stop. Don't move." His voice sounded strange. It never occurred to me to say "Why?" or to argue or not obey. I froze where I was.

After a long moment a snake emerged from under the wheelbarrow and slithered across the ground not a foot away from me. By that time I could not have moved if I'd wanted to. It was a fairly small snake with shiny bands of red and yellow. He went past me and disappeared in the grass.

"What was it?" I could hardly hear myself speak.

"Coral snake."

I was out of that field and running down the road without even stopping to feel ashamed of myself. I ran so hard, I came around a bend and almost smashed into Felicité. She looked angry.

[76]

"What you do, you? Where you go?"

I tried to calm down. "We were just wandering around."

She wagged her bony finger at me. "You stay out of da fields, you get snake-bit. You hear me?"

"Okay. All right."

"Okay all right', yah. Me. I tell you good, you stay away from here. Where your brother?"

Where, indeed? I turned around, suddenly panicked. Had the snake got him, after all? But there he was, coming along the road much more slowly than I had. He looked pale, and he had a strange expression on his face, sort of dazed. Felicité went through her act all over again for Franklin's benefit, but he just nodded absentmindedly and said, "Yeah, all right."

We walked up the road till we came to the white iron bench where we had first seen Eva.

"Let's sit down a minute," Franklin said. "I don't feel so good."

"You don't look so good. You didn't get bitten, did you?"

"No. No, it wasn't that."

Felicité had not come back. "What was Felicité all wrought up about, do you think. Does she care that much if a snake bites us?"

"I suppose Eva would blame her if anything

happened to us." He said it, but I didn't think he was paying much attention to what he was saying.

"What's the matter?"

He leaned back and thrust his hands into his pockets as if he were trying to get a hold on himself. "After Felicité, or whoever, cleaned up the potting shed, something was missing. I couldn't think what it was, didn't really give it much thought." He paused.

"So?"

"I've remembered. It was an old chest, like Grandpa's father's sea chest, with iron hinges. The first day we explored, I looked inside. It was just junk, old tools and stuff. Like the things we found in the garçonnière later."

"What about it?"

"It disappeared after François's . . . accident. I just found it."

I sat up straight. "Found it where?"

"In the ground. In that place that looked dug up, near the wheelbarrow."

"You mean it's buried there?"

"Yeah. When you see it like that, it looks like . . . like a coffin."

Now *I* felt sick. "Did you open it?"

"I couldn't. I need a shovel to get the dirt off it." He turned and looked at me. "Tonight after it's dark I'm going to sneak out there and look."

"After dark! Franklin, you are not."

"I am. You see what happens in the daylight. Felicité is watching us."

"But Franklin, not in the dark. Let's just tell Mom and Ian and let them deal with it."

"Oh, sure. First, we'd catch hell for going down there. Second, they wouldn't believe us. Third . . . well, third, I'm going to look myself before I tell anybody. If I'm wrong, then nobody gets to bawl me out or laugh at me or whatever."

"But snakes, Franklin."

"I'll get the flashlight out of the car."

I thought about it a long time. "If you go, I'm going with you."

"Oh, no."

"Oh, yes."

"Sis, no. You'd panic and run. Just like you did now."

"No, I won't. I swear. And anyway I didn't yell." I was pleased that he'd called me Sis. He hadn't used that old nickname for a long time.

"You've never seen a dead body."

"Neither have you."

He was silent. I could see the outline of his fists clenched in the tight jeans pockets. "All right," he said, "but you have to let me go first, and if I tell you not to look, you won't look. And don't tell."

I promised.

ALL THROUGH DINNER that night I kept thinking we really ought to tell Mom, but I had promised. We could tell her afterward if anything was there. It must just be an old box full of junk, after all, maybe stuff Felicité wanted to throw away. Why bury it though? I tried not to ask myself questions. Tonight would give us the answers.

We agreed to sneak out the kitchen door at midnight sharp. Ian and Mom would be asleep by then, most likely. Franklin had found the flashlight in the car glove compartment and smuggled it up to his room. And he had checked to make sure the shovel was still in the potting shed. We allegedly went to bed at the usual hour.

Midnight was a long time coming, and at the same time it came too fast. At about quarter of, I got up and put on two pairs of wool socks and the thickest pair of shoes I had, which weren't very thick. In summer, after all, you don't wear big boots. I tucked the legs of my jeans inside my socks, put on a long-sleeved shirt, and wound my hair in a knot and tied it back with a scarf. It looked weird, but this was one time when I wasn't interested in how I looked.

I let myself out of my room and went on tiptoe down the hall to the back stairs. By this time I knew which boards squeaked, and I avoided them. Franklin was already standing by the kitchen door waiting for me.

We went out, leaving the door unlatched. The doors all had enormous locks, but nobody had ever locked them while we were there.

We walked single file in the dark past the wing, being very careful. I had the feeling that Felicité could hear our hearts beat at a hundred paces. Franklin got the shovel from the potting shed.

When we were clear of all the outbuildings, Franklin turned on the flash, and we walked side by side, watching the path just in case.

I whispered, "What if we miss the turn?"

He shook his head. "I marked it."

My brother. He'd make a good private eye, or an Indian scout.

When we came to the turnoff, it took all the nerve I had to make myself step over the ditch into that field. It had been bad enough in daylight, but now . . . "Aren't snakes nocturnal?" I said.

"Forget about snakes."

"Oh, sure."

"Just watch where you step. They aren't going to come into the path of the light."

When we got close to the place, he handed me the light. "You stand here and flash the light onto the . . . the dug-up place."

I was sure he had almost said "grave." I took

the light from him and felt how icy cold his hands were. He was probably as scared as I was, but that wouldn't stop him. And it was not going to stop me either. But I was weak with fright.

He started digging. I fervently hoped Felicité wasn't sitting up in bed with her supersonic ear turned toward us, because that shovel did clink a lot. The ground was heavy and damp and hard to dig. I heard Franklin grunt with effort as he heaved away shovelfuls of earth. Then the metal struck something hard.

"Move the light in a little."

I took knee-high steps toward him, though I didn't know what good I thought that did.

"There. Hold it." He began to dig away at the edges of the box. After a while he leaned over. He had to do some prying with the edge of the shovel, but suddenly a corner of the chest gave way, and he pried it up. He said, "Oh, God," in a sick voice. I started toward him, but he said, "Stay where you are." He threw the shovel into the weeds and grabbed the flashlight, "Let's go."

I couldn't keep up with him. He was soon so far ahead of me, the light did me no good, and I was floundering along in the grass trying not to think of snakes. I almost screamed when a heavy wet strand of Spanish moss hit me in the face, and I didn't see the ditch in time to jump it. My feet sank ankle-deep in mud and silt. A moth bumped against my cheek. I tried to tell Franklin to wait, but I was too scared to speak.

Then a voice right behind me said, "Good evening," and a big bony hand clamped down on my shoulder.

7

I SHRIEKED. Promise or no promise, I shrieked. Franklin said, "What's the matter?" in a scared voice.

A beam of light shone on both of us. A voice said, "What on earth are you kids doing out here in the middle of the night?"

It was Arthur. I nearly collapsed with relief. My knees shook so hard, if he hadn't still had hold of my shoulder, I'd have fallen right down in a heap.

"Who is it?" Franklin still sounded scared to death.

"It's only me. Arthur." For a second he shone the light on himself. I saw that he was quite a lot older than I had imagined. Though he was tanned and fit-looking, his face had lines around the mouth and eyes. He looked amused, and at that moment amusement seemed to me to be about the least appropriate reaction anybody could have. I began to feel angry.

"What are you doing here?" I said.

He chuckled. "That was my question to you. But I'll answer first. My sister told me there was a night-blooming cereus out here in the field. I was trying to find it. You scared the daylights out of me, I might add." He had a nice voice and I began to feel a little more relaxed.

"I forgot, you don't know my brother; Franklin, this is Arthur."

Franklin ignored the introduction. "Your sister?" he said.

"Yes, Eva."

"Eva is your *sister?*"

"Yes. Is that so amazing?"

"Yes. We thought . . . we didn't know you were her brother."

"Ah, you thought I was the paramour." He laughed. "What a funny idea. Dear old Eva."

It *was* a funny idea, when you thought of it.

"Now. What were you doing?"

"My sister lost her bracelet when we were out here a couple of days ago," Franklin said. He was shading his eyes against Arthur's light, so I couldn't see his face. "Our mother asked about it tonight at dinner, so we figured we'd better find it quick. It's a sort of family heirloom, and she'd really be mad . . ."

"Wouldn't it have been better to search in daylight?"

"We were pretty sure where she dropped it."

Arthur had somehow turned us around and was walking us toward the house.

"And did you find it?"

"No. My sister got scared. She worries about snakes."

It was a dirty trick, turning me into a sissy, but I knew Franklin was doing the best he could. Doing pretty well, all things considered.

"Did you find your cereus?" I asked.

"No, darn it. I seem to have missed it. It only blooms one night in the year, you know. I couldn't find it at all, blooming or un-." He was really being rather nice. Certainly friendly. At the approach to our back door, he said, "Better luck next time. With your bracelet." And he disappeared in the dark.

In the house Franklin and I stared at each other, trying to read each other's faces.

"Night-blooming cereus," he said, "is a cactus. I don't think it would grow in a wet place like that field."

"What did you find?" I said.

He sighed. "François."

I grabbed the kitchen table for support, and a knife fell to the floor with a clatter. "What'll we do?"

"In the morning we'll tell Mom, and she and Ian can go to the police."

"Do you think Arthur knows?"

"I don't think Arthur was looking for flowers." He put his finger to his lips.

Mom called down the stairs. "Franklin? Dorothy?"

"We'd better tell her now," I said.

We met her on the stairs. She looked appalled. "What in the world! Were you *outside?* You're all muddy."

"Mother, come into my room and sit down. We have something to tell you."

She sat on my bed and listened. When we had finished, she said, "How awful. How dreadful. What can have happened? It doesn't make sense." She didn't wait for answers. "In the morning we'll go to the police. We'd never be able to find anybody tonight in that little village. You two had better come, too. Be up early. And, please, darlings, no more adventures, not on your own. You could get hurt, and I could not bear it."

We were both up at dawn, sitting in the kitchen drinking hot chocolate, trying to make some sense out of everything. We got nowhere. Who would want to hide the fact that poor old François was dead? Had someone killed him? What for? None of the reasons that you find in mystery stories seemed to apply. In Agatha Christie, people killed for inheritances, or for love, or something like that. Old François simply didn't fit.

Mother looked as if she hadn't slept, and Ian looked as if he had not waked up.

"You chaps are absolutely sure, are you?" he said. "I mean, it sounds so frightfully implausible."

He was right, it did, but I wished he would believe us now and then.

"We're sure," Franklin said grimly.

"Yes, well, we'd better get right on into the village. Eva isn't here, is she?"

"Arthur is," I said.

Franklin went outside and came back in a minute. "No, he isn't. His car is gone."

"Probably gone to work," Ian said. "He's a tennis pro, you know. At some club or other in the city."

"Should we speak to Felicité?" Mother said.

Franklin and I answered in one breath, "No."

"Should I go have a look . . . uhh . . ." Ian tapered off.

Franklin shrugged. "You can if you want to. That field is full of snakes. A coral snake practically walked over Dorothy's feet yesterday."

My mother gasped and looked pale. I suddenly realized how much she really did worry about us. I patted her hand, and she gave me a wan smile.

"Well, let's go then," Ian said. He seemed impatient, as if we had made up the whole thing. Perhaps I might have felt the same. I wished I could say so, but I didn't know how to say it. I wasn't enough at ease with him.

It took us a while to find the policeman, who seemed to be head honcho in the village. In fact, as far as we ever found out, he was the only cop in town, and he was the law only when his services were required. We found him in his gas station, pumping unleaded into somebody's Toyota.

When he was free, he took us into the gas station and said, "Now. What can I do for you?" He seemed like a nice guy, maybe thirty-five years old, tall and fairly rugged, with a complexion that looked Spanish to me. Mom said later that he was a Creole, but I don't really know what that means.

Ian started things off, saying, "The youngsters here have a rather extraordinary story that we think you ought to hear."

Mother picked up from there, explaining who we were and why we were in the area. Then she looked at Franklin, "All right, son, tell your story."

I hated the way they kept saying "your story." True, it was a crazy story, even Mom sounded as if she wasn't sure, and she should have known we wouldn't make it up. I was proud of my brother though. Without going into any unnecessary detail, he told the man what had happened, from the time François crashed into the house, to our finding him out cold, to what Felicité said, and so on, through the finding of the body and the meeting with Arthur.

The policeman, whose name was George, frowned. "I know Arthur and Eva. Been living around here all my life." He stared hard at the blotter on his little desk. "Odd story. Well, let's go have a look." He hung a CLOSED sign in the doorway, locked up, and followed us out to the plantation.

Nobody was saying much. When we got out of the two cars, we led him and Mom and Ian down the dirt road to the field.

"Why don't you ladies stay here," Ian said. "No sense getting all mucked up in that mud."

With Franklin leading the way, he and the policeman followed to the place where the burial had taken place.

Mom said, "Oh, I can't stand this, snakes or no snakes." And she jumped the ditch and went after them, so I went too.

I saw Franklin staring at the place in a puzzled way. Then I saw why. The digging he had done the night before had been filled in and the whole area seemed lower. The chest was not in sight. Dirt had been scattered over the spot so that you wouldn't think anything had happened there, except that maybe an animal had been digging around and had loosened up the ground.

"Where was it, son?" the policeman said. He scooched down beside the place.

"Right here. Wait, I'll get the shovel, but someone has been here. It all looks different." Franklin went into the long grass and came back a minute later. "The shovel's gone." His face looked tight and and pale. "I threw the shovel down there last night, but it's gone."

The policeman began kicking away the dirt, first with his boot, then with a stick. Franklin helped him, and I could see he was frantic.

The policeman thrust the stick down through the dirt. Then he looked up at Franklin. "We'll need a shovel," he said, "but there doesn't seem to be anything there now."

The usually mild expression on Ian's face was gone. He looked as black as a thundercloud, and I knew what he was thinking. "Franklin, get a shovel," he snapped. "Quick."

Franklin gave me a desperate look and ran off to get a shovel.

George, the policeman, seemed unconcerned.

[*91*]

He looked at me and smiled and said in his soft southern drawl, "Did you happen to see this chest or box, too?"

"Well, no," I said. "Franklin wouldn't let me look. It was too scary."

Ian's mouth tightened into a thin line.

"But it was there all right," I said. "Franklin was as white as a sheet."

"And Arthur DuPré," George said, "did he see this chest?"

"I don't know what Arthur saw. He caught up with us out in the road."

"But he didn't mention it?"

"No. He said he was looking for a night-blooming cereus."

George's eyebrows shot up. "And .you didn't mention it to him."

"Well, no. We didn't know . . . I mean we thought you ought to be told first."

He smiled. "Eh, you did the right thing."

Franklin came racing back with a shovel and gave it to George. Franklin exchanged glances with me. "Yeah," he said, "it's the same shovel. I know by the dent in it."

George dug carefully. When the grave was laid open, it held nothing but loose dirt, trash, broken branches. He straightened up. "No chest."

I was afraid Franklin was going to cry, though

I hadn't seen him cry for about six years.

"It was there," he muttered.

"Well, Inspector," Ian said, "we apologize for bringing you out here on a wild goose chase." He shot a black look at us. "We accepted the story. I should have checked."

"Oh, no," George said. "Me, I am the one to check these things out. You did quite right." He handed the shovel back to Franklin and gave him a reassuring pat. George was a really nice man.

Mom asked him to come in and have coffee, and he did. I wondered if he minded losing business at the gas station, but it didn't seem to bother him. He praised my mother's coffee.

"Good dark roast. You know how to make it the Louisiana way."

Mom looked pleased. She had avoided saying anything at all about the missing chest. I could tell she was puzzled. She does know us well enough to know we don't tell lies, no matter what our other bad habits may be. And I could see now that she wasn't doubting us. She was just trying to figure it out. I was relieved that she still trusted us.

When George had gone, Ian turned on us like a smash of thunder. Gone were the diffident smile, the mild-looking expression in his eyes. He was furious. Even his voice was different.

"Now then, Franklin," he said.

"Ian," Mom said, but he ignored her. She looked upset, not with us, but with Ian. I caught her hand to stop her from saying anything. There was no use in her fighting with Ian over us.

"You've been wanting to humiliate me ever since we met. You resent me because your mother loves me. I knew it would be like this. Children always hate stepparents."

"But we don't," I said, but he wasn't about to listen.

"You've made me look like an utter fool in front of the police. Now go to your rooms, both of you."

We went. Franklin hadn't said a word in his defense. As we went up the stairs, I could hear Mom and Ian talking, and it sounded like an argument.

At the top of the stairs, Franklin said quietly, "I may have been rude to him, but I didn't make it up about François. He was there, and now he isn't."

"Of course, I know you didn't make it up." It surprised me that he had to explain that to me.

He went into his room and closed the door, and I didn't see him again until the next day.

8

WE MADE A POINT of staying out of Ian's way after that, and Mom seemed to aid and abet us by fixing meals for us at odd hours, without complaining, and things like that. She was unusually quiet, and sometimes I caught her studying us. I had a feeling she had tuned into our wavelength, about the mystery of François. But it was all perfectly clear to Ian: François had gotten drunk and had an accident and passed out. When he recovered, he had gone to visit his sister. Arthur had been looking for a night-blooming cereus, and we had arranged an elaborate practical joke to make Ian look silly. Clear as a geometry theorem. But I knew Mom didn't buy that. I could almost see the little cogs in her brain whirring. But she said nothing about it and we said nothing. She went out of her way to treat Franklin like an adult, and I could tell he was grateful. He even hugged her once or twice, and Franklin is not big on hugging.

Arthur had not been around since that night, but that was not unusual. He seemed to come mostly on weekends; Eva, too. She was there more than he, we thought, but she seemed always to be just on the periphery of our vision, always just disappearing, like smoke. When we saw her, she looked witchier than ever, and several times we felt she was glaring at us from a distance.

We went over to Justin's several times and went out with him in his nice, faded blue, fish-smelling boat. We'd just drift along near the shore, in and out of the inlets, the boys fishing, me lying on my back with my hat pulled down over my eyes, just enjoying myself and sometimes thinking. It was very peaceful.

One afternoon Franklin said, "I'm glad we're here with you, Justin. If I had to find my way in this maze, I'd never make it."

Justin laughed. "That's why the pirates liked it so good. They could just hide out, easy as easy."

I heard the splash of his line in the water. After a minute he began to reel in, but it turned out to be part of an old inner tube. Disgusted, he tossed it back. "Everything's in this river, man, every kinda junk. Said on the radio the police found a body last night, downriver a ways."

I opened my eyes. "A body?"

"Yeah. They're always finding bodies. Guys get drunk and fall in, or somebody . . ." He made a gesture of cutting a throat. "Into the river. Nobody ever knows."

Franklin was looking at me. He said, "I wonder if George knows about the body."

"What George?" Justin said.

"The policeman."

"Oh, George. Sure he knows. He was down there first thing, soon as the guys let him know what they found."

I was sitting up. "Did they know who the body was?"

"Nope. They never know. Old man river and all them fish, it don't take long to quit looking like yourself"

I saw Franklin's shudder. "Maybe we better be getting back," he said.

Justin gave a lazy laugh. "You scared you'll fall in? Don't worry. I'd fish you out."

But we went in soon afterward and walked home in silence. Finally Franklin said, "Do you think it could be?"

"I don't know. I'm sick of all the questions I don't know answers to. If it was, George can handle it. He knew François."

Franklin smiled, the first time in several days. "What kind of a Miss Marple would you make?"

"Terrible."

At the entrance to the long alley leading to Belle Rêve, we paused as we always did now, to glance in the big mailbox that sometimes held a newspaper (although Ian usually got to it first) or an advertising flyer. Once there had been a letter for us from Grandma, which we had answered the same day. Today there was only a flyer from an appliance store in New Orleans.

Franklin stood looking at it, and I was sure he was not thinking about twenty-four-inch color television now marked down, down, down, or the upright freezer for all your delicious summer produce.

"What is it?" I said.

"Have you got a pencil?"

I found a stub of a pencil in my jeans pocket and gave it to him. He spread the flyer out on top of the mail box and carefully printed in large letters: HE HAS BEEN FOUND. Then he stuffed the flyer into the other box, where the mail for Eva and Arthur went.

"What's that all about?" I said.

He shrugged. "Maybe it will stir something up."

"You think it was François in the river."

Again he shrugged. "You just said it a minute ago, all questions, no answers."

I didn't know what he expected his "message" to do, but he didn't seem to want to be cross-examined, so I let him alone. Maybe it was just something to do, not a real plan at all.

When we got home, Mom had just come in from painting. I went into the kitchen and looked at her watercolor and was startled to see Jasmine in it. "Is she back?"

"Jasmine? No, not that I know of. That's the painting I started when she was still here. I was working on it today from memory." She squinted at it. It showed Jasmine in her crazy high bonnet and her long purple dress looking like something out of some old trunk. She was stooping over a little, looking at something in her hand, maybe a flower, and she was posed against the side of one of the brick slave quarters.

"That's François's house," I said.

"Yes," Mom murmured, as if she were thinking about something else. She propped the painting on the table, against the sugar bowl, and studied it. "I wish she hadn't run away. She's a marvelous subject."

"What has she got in her hand?"

"I don't know. I couldn't see. As soon as she saw me, she threw whatever it was into the doorway of the house and sped off as if the devil were after her."

"Didn't you look at what she threw in the house?"

"Of course not." She gave me a mildly re-proachful look. "It was somebody else's house, after all."

I noticed she said "was," but that just might have been good English, not a statement of any kind of fact. She's careful about grammar.

"Anyway, Felicité came by later and picked it up and put it in a table drawer. I heard the drawer slam."

I grinned. Mom might draw the line at trespassing, but she didn't miss much.

"It's funny François doesn't come back, if he's all right." It was the first remark I'd tried out on her about all that.

She didn't look at me, just said, very softly, "Curioser and curioser." And she went upstairs.

I told Franklin about the painting later on and the mysterious object that Jasmine had thrown into François's house. After dinner we went for a little walk down the "street," as Justin said the path was called where the slave quarters were.

Nobody seemed to be around. We stopped in front of François's place. The door was ajar, and a nasty-looking roach skittered across the dirt floor. I really hate roaches, they make me sick to look at them. I turned away and was leaving, but Franklin went in.

"Franklin, you'll get in trouble."

"Just killing a roach," he said. His voice from inside the old brick house sounded hollow. "Mom hates roaches. Just helping her exterminate, that's all." There was a thud, which I tried not to hear. "Got him," Franklin called out.

He didn't come out, and finally I couldn't stand the suspense. I went to the door and looked in. "What are you doing?"

"Just snooping."

It didn't seem like a fertile field for snooping. There was an iron cot with a sagging mattress, a table with canted legs, a couple of old kitchen chairs, a twelve-inch black and white TV that wasn't connected to anything. On the table there was an oil lamp with a chimney that needed cleaning. An armoire stood tilted on the uneven floor, its doors hanging open, revealing a couple of pairs of overalls wadded up and thrown on the floor, an old pair of shoes, a shirt. Poor François. I wondered how he happened to end up like this.

Franklin looked under the bed and kicked out a couple of empty whiskey bottles.

"Let's get out of here," I said. "It's depressing."

He tried the small drawer in the table. It stuck.

"Franklin, come on."

"You don't have to stay." He got out his Scout

knife and worked on the drawer. It's funny how patiently boys will do something like that. Personally, I'd give it a yank, and if it stuck, I'd leave it.

The drawer flew open, and an empty snuffbox fell out. Franklin bent down and peered inside the drawer. Methodically he took out the contents, item by item. A mildewed change purse with nothing in it; an empty pack of cigarettes; a rusty knife; a can opener; a cancelled train ticket. I was inside the room now, but I was getting more and more nervous. "Let's go, come on."

"Wait. There's a snapshot or something . . . It's caught in the side of the drawer . . ." He had his knife out again.

"Franklin! Someone's coming."

He scooped up all the stuff and dumped it back in the drawer and closed it.

"It's Félicité. We can't get out without being seen." I was really terrified, without knowing exactly why.

He grabbed my arm and dragged me inside the big armoire, pulling the door shut. I thought I would die right then and there. We were squeezed up against the back of the armoire, with just enough room to stand. Our heads bumped the shelf. The thing stank of dirty clothes and mildew, and I was sure it must be full of cockroaches and spiders and, for all I knew, snakes.

Franklin had a tight grip on my wrist. We heard Felicité step inside the room. What if she wanted something from the armoire? I tried to think what I would do if she opened the door and saw us jammed in there.

We could hear her moving around the room, but we couldn't tell what she was doing. She must have seen us go down the path, though I could only hope she hadn't seen us step in here.

Franklin's grip on my wrist tightened as we heard the scrape of the drawer in the table. He had shoved it shut, and she seemed to be trying to open it. After a minute the noise stopped. She went out and shut the door behind her.

Cautiously Franklin opened the armoire door, and I almost fell out. One more minute in there, and I would have fainted for sure. He looked at the drawer and grinned.

"She couldn't open it."

"Franklin, we are leaving. This minute." I grabbed his arm and pulled him out of there.

"All right," he said, "but as soon as I can, I'm coming back to look at that old snapshot."

9

_____

IT SEEMED AS IF we could not move for the next
couple of days without coming across Felicité or
Arthur or Eva. Franklin's message had been removed
from the mailbox, and they must have guessed one of
us had left it. I wondered what they made of it.
You couldn't actually prove they were watching
us, but I was sure they were keeping close track.
Arthur usually said something cheerful and non-
committal, like, "Beautiful day for ducks." This was
supposedly a joke; it had rained all night, and the
trees dripped steadily, like Queen Niobe weeping
for her fourteen children. Or he would say, "Tell
your dad I have a carving to show him." Didn't he
know Ian was not our father?

When we saw Eva, she mostly didn't see us.
She seemed more preoccupied than ever, her face

all screwed up in wrinkles of worry. She could have been worried about her mother's having gone bonkers again; but she could also have been worried about something else.

The third day, Sunday, we had a break. We saw Felicité get into a very ancient Ford with an old man and an old lady as little and mean-looking as she was, and we watched them drive away. Neither Arthur nor Eva was in sight, so we went directly to François's house.

I had to force myself to go back in there, and I told Franklin that if anybody caught us this time, they'd just have to catch me, because I would rather die than step into that stinking armoire again.

"We'll only be a minute," Franklin said. "You keep watch."

I stood in the doorway, feeling nervous, while Franklin struggled with the drawer again. He had closed it so tight the other day that it was really stuck this time, and he had to work and work at it with the blade of his knife. It seemed to take forever. I was about to say, "Let's get out of here." After all, why did we care about an old snapshot? But before I could say it, the drawer flew open, the same as it had before, spilling out the things on top.

I heard Franklin say, "Here it comes." And then there was a silence, and then he whistled, a low surprised whistle. I turned around and said, "What?"

"Take a look at this."

I went over to him and took the snapshot from his hand. I had to hold it up to the light to see it. It had faded out to browns and almost whites. But I could make out a man, young, in what looked like a pair of white cotton pants and a striped sweater. With him was a girl in a calf-length frilly dress and one of those big picture hats they used to wear. "Is it François?"

"Sure. Here, let me hold it so you can see it better." He held it in a different light. "Look at the girl."

I looked. It was Jasmine. It had to be. I'd know those eyes anywhere. "Jasmine." I said.

"Right. François, Jasmine, with their arms around each other, cozy as can be. What does that tell you?"

"She was carrying on with the gardener?"

"Remember what Justin's grandfather said? When you asked if François ever married? He said, 'They don' low that,' and then he said, 'Masta, he run him off.' "

We stared at each other. "You mean," I said, "Jasmine and François were in love? And her father ran him off? But he's here . . . *was* here."

"He might have come back after Jasmine's old man died."

[*106*]

"What about Jasmine's husband? I mean, if she had two children, she must have had a husband. Or something."

"Mom said Eva told her that her father died when Eva was a real little kid. That's how come the place sort of got rundown."

"But Arthur . . ."

"Arthur must have been away a lot. There are pictures of him, and of Eva too, in an old album in the bottom drawer of the bureau in my room. One of them shows him about my age, in a school military uniform, and then there are some of him in an Army uniform. He was a second lieutenant, and he had an artillery insignia on his collar. Maybe Korea. Hard to tell."

"You never told me."

"I didn't know you'd be interested. I'm interested in war stuff. Well, let's keep this picture and think about what it means, if anything."

A cool, drawly voice from behind us said, "I'll just take that off your hands if you don't mind."

We whirled around, and there stood Arthur, in white tennis shorts and a white T-shirt and sneakers, the smiling and gracious tennis pro. He held out his hand.

Franklin put his hands behind his back. "We found it," he said. "Finders keepers."

"Hardly 'found,'" Arthur said. "More like ran-sacking, looting, stealing, wouldn't you say? This is not your house, after all."

"It isn't yours, either," Franklin said. His jaw was stuck out, the way it gets when he's not going to give in.

"Come, come," Arthur said, beginning to sound impatient. "This *is* our plantation, you know. I'd like that snapshot, if you don't mind."

"What has happened to François?" I said.

He looked almost convincingly puzzled. "Hap-pened to him? He's visiting his sister, I understand."

"Where?" I said.

He gave an elaborate shrug, as if we were being really too boring. "I don't keep track of our gar-dener's kin. Somewhere up the river, I presume."

"François doesn't have a sister," I said, "and he comes from Cajun country."

For a second his composure slipped. Then he got it back and said, "How charming of you to in-form yourselves about our help. You Yankees have such a keen interest in the lower classes." He held out his hand. "The picture, please."

"I'm sorry," Franklin said, "but I'm not going to give it to you."

"Oh? May one ask what you think you're going to do with it?"

"I'm going to give it to the cop, to George. I think he might be interested."

"George?" He laughed. "Why on earth should he want a snapshot of François?"

"You did know it was a picture of François?" I said.

Again he looked disconcerted for a moment.

Franklin said, "Because François seems to have disappeared. The police are interested."

"Indeed." And then as Franklin stepped forward, to go out the door, Arthur blocked the doorway, and suddenly in his hand was the tiniest gun I've ever seen. I found out afterward it was a derringer, but right then I thought he was trying to bluff us with a toy, a water pistol or something. Until I looked at Franklin and saw in his face that he did not think it was a toy. He had turned white.

Then things happened so fast, it's hard to sort them out now in the right order. A shadow loomed up behind Arthur, Arthur turned quickly, with the gun now pointing right at Ian, who was the shadow. Ian was red in the face, and he was saying in his crazy tea-party English voice, "Put that thing down, old man." And Arthur said, "Get out of here. I don't want to hurt anyone." So Ian suddenly ducked sideways, crouched, and tackled Arthur around the waist. The gun went off, and I screamed, and Franklin thrust the snapshot into my hand and landed on Arthur from behind. For a minute all you could see was thrashing arms and legs, and then the gun flew out of Arthur's hand and quick as a flash Ian pounced on it.

"Get up," he said to Arthur, who by this time was flat on his back.

Arthur got up, brushing off his clothes, trying to look cool but not succeeding at all.

By this time both Eva and my mother had arrived, having heard the gunshot. Eva was weeping hysterically and wringing her hands, and Mom was looking at Ian with an almost beaming look of pride.

Keeping the gun on Arthur, Ian said, "Dorothy, run to the house and call George."

I ran to the house, looked up the number and called. All the time I could hear Eva crying, "No, no, no!" I got George right away and told him he'd better come in a hurry.

George doesn't look as if he ever did anything in a hurry, but he was there sooner than I'd have thought possible. He sauntered down the "street" to this little tableau that was still holding in place. "Well, well," he said. "What's up?"

"They're mad." Eva was sobbing. "Get them off my property. I'll return the rent. George, get rid of them."

George took the derringer from Ian and looked

it over as if he were examining a rare work of art. "Pretty little thing," he said finally. "Why don't you"—he nodded to Ian—"and Arthur come on down to the station house and we'll have ourselves a talk. And you, Miss Eva, you go in the house and fix yourself a good stiff drink—one of those Sazeracs your mother used to be famous for—and try to get a hold of yourself."

Ian said, "Righto, old chap, but I think my stepchildren have something you ought to have. Dorothy, let George have the picture." He smiled at my mother. "I don't know what it is, but the children risked their bloody necks to get it, and Arthur produced his gun to get it away from them, so I presume it's important."

I gave the snapshot to George, who put it carefully in his wallet without really looking at it. Eva gave another shriek and cried out, "Oh, no!"

"Ma'am," George said to my mother, "give Miss Eva a hand up to the house, would you? If there are any tranquillizers in the medicine cabinet, and I'll bet there are, see that she takes one." He patted Eva on the shoulder. "Take it easy, Miss Eva, take it easy. It'll all come out in the wash."

My mother led sobbing Eva away, and the men went off with George. Franklin and I looked at each other.

"Everybody gets into the act but us," he said.

"And we're the ones that find all the clues."

I was thinking about Ian. "Ian could have gotten killed."

"I know. The way he acted was very professional, very cool. Was he ever in the war?"

"I don't know."

He sighed. "He risked his life for us, you might say."

"You might say that."

10

THEY WERE GONE a long time. Mom stayed over in the wing with Eva, and Franklin and I were left to ourselves. Finally just because we couldn't stand sitting around and waiting for something to happen, we strolled down the road to Justin's place. We didn't say anything about all that had been going on, partly because we couldn't explain any of it yet, and partly because we had gotten the feeling that Justin and his grandfather would prefer not to do much gossiping about the DuPrés or any of their neighbors. For the first time it occurred to me that it might have been difficult for them when their "Michie" left his plantation to his black workers. I could imagine white plantation people not being happy with that, any more than they were happy in the old days when the slaves were freed. It meant the end of their way of life, and I suppose to them that would have been a tragedy. You had only to look at how rundown and even abandoned a lot of the big places were to realize the upheavals that had taken place over the years.

Justin did volunteer one piece of information, which I guess he thought would be public knowledge anyway. He said, "They found out who that was they fished out of the river."

"Who?" We asked the question together.

"Old François."

It was what we had expected, but still it was a shock to have it verified. Poor old François.

"They figure he got drunk and fell in," Justin said. "The old man hardly ever was sober, not for years and years."

"I wonder why," Franklin said. "I mean there's usually a reason, isn't there, when people become alcoholics?"

Justin shrugged, and we could see he wasn't going to offer any more thoughts on the subject. "Some folks drink, like, I mean they just drink." And then he started telling us about some crawdads he and his grandfather had caught the day before. "Grandpère made some hushpuppies to go with 'em, and we had us a fine meal." He rubbed his flat stomach.

We were too itchy to know what was happening to stay long. And when we came in sight of the house, we broke into a run.

Sure enough, when we burst into the house, Ian was just back. He gave us a long look that I couldn't figure out, and then he said, "Sit down, you chaps. I'll bring you up to date."

Needless to say, we sat down and gave him our total attention.

"It's rather a complicated story really, and it starts years back. It seems François worked here as a young man, and he and Jasmine fell in love. Her father was outraged, of course, and ran the chap off. Jasmine married a suitable fellow, who unfortunately died a number of years later." He paused and looked at us. "Possibly you already know this?"

"We sort of figured it out," Franklin said.

Ian raised his eyebrows and looked at Mom. "Remarkable. Well, with both her husband and her father off the scene, as it were, Jasmine either summoned François or he turned up and she let him stay. The situation was a bit ambiguous. I gather that for a time he actually lived in the other wing, the one that's now empty; but he and Jasmine apparently had some prodigious quarrels, and eventually he was banished to the slave quarters." He stopped and cleared his throat. "It was rather an unconventional situation. You see, there was Eva, child of Jasmine and Mr.

DuPré. And there was . . . uh . . . Arthur . . ."
He paused again.

I let out a yelp. "Child of Jasmine and François!"

"Precisely. I see I have managed to surprise you
at last. Yes, Arthur was the wood's colt, as they say.
But he was brought up and treated exactly as Eva
was, all the privileges and perks, and society at large
seems to have accepted it. Forgot it, even. Of course
there's not much 'society' out here."

"But Felicité remembered . . ." Franklin began.

"Felicité did. She had been Jasmine's servant and
devoted companion since Jasmine was a young girl.
No doubt she was her confidante as well. There
seems to have been nothing Felicité didn't know and
wouldn't do for her lady."

"Even to killing François?" I said.

"Oh no, no, Felicité didn't kill anyone, though
I'm sure she is capable of it."

"Then who . . ." I began.

"The night that poor François mowed the grass
in his drunken exuberance, and incidentally dam-
aged part of the house, he and Jasmine had the row
of all time. Jasmine, as you know, has been in a nursing home. Her mind has slipped a bit, I gather. After
Felicité conveyed the bruised and sodden François
to the slave quarters, Jasmine crept out of the house

[116]

unnoticed and took up the fight again. Somehow they ended up in the potting shed—possibly poor François was trying to get away from her—anyway she conked him on the head with the hoe and knocked him out. This alarmed her. She saw a whiskey bottle lying about and apparently gave François a hefty swig. Unfortunately it turned out to be some sort of pesticide. She left him there, not knowing she had done him in."

"Then we happened along," Franklin said.

"Right. And found the *corpus delicti*, but didn't know it was one. Or did you?"

"Not really, but we kind of worried about it."

"Precisely. Well, then, you told Felicité, and she found him dead as a dodo and right away guessed what had happened. At nightfall she trundled him off in the wheelbarrow and buried him.

"And put the incriminating evidence in the garçonnière," Franklin said.

Ian looked at him thoughtfully, and then at Mom. "There may be something to be said for overzealousness. Yes, she tried to make it look as if the old man had just gone away. To protect her lady, you see. She told Arthur and Eva, and Eva hustled Mama back to the safety of the nursing home. But not before Jasmine had tossed the photo of François and herself into his cabin. Who knows why? Perhaps to get rid of it, perhaps because in her addled brain she was rejecting him one more time. All of them, needless to say, were upset."

"And Arthur wasn't looking for a night-blooming cereus, he was looking for François," Franklin said. "To bury him some place where Yankee kids wouldn't go snooping."

"Exactly. Not to put too fine a point on it, he dumped the body in the bayou. It later was washed up, but if you two hadn't alerted George, it would have gone unidentified. George had a dental check made, and it tallied. Arthur's main concern was to keep you from finding out any more. They kept a close watch on you. When Felicité was sure someone had been messing with the drawer in François's table, she remembered the snapshot. She had thought it would be safe there, I suppose. What they were afraid of, you see, was not only that their poor old mother would be accused of a murder she hadn't meant to commit, but it seems that Arthur is engaged to one of his tennis students, a rich widow and a lady of impeccable New Orleans background. Having it come out that he was illegitimate, and all the rest of the sordid little story, did not suit his purpose at all. So he got just a touch desperate." He tipped his chair back. "I believe that's the whole story."

"Except," Mother said, "that I found the trunk,

poor François's coffin. It's half buried in the vegetable garden."

We were silent, taking it all in. "How did George ever get Arthur to tell all that?" Franklin said. "Did he torture him?"

Ian smiled. "No. But George has lived here all his life, and he has a shrewd way of putting two and two together and getting the other person to come up with four. I've never seen a more skillful questioning. It was like a relaxed social conversation, but he got everything he needed."

"And a signed statement?" Franklin asked.

"And a signed statement." Ian gave us a long look. "I do want to say that I owe you chaps an apology. Several apologies, in fact. I failed to be at all understanding about your feelings towards me. I was so eager to have you accept me, don't you know, I expected too much, and at the same time was sure I wouldn't get it. I grew up with a stepmother whom I loathed. I thought you were pulling my leg about the body in the cane field and all the rest of it. I do apologize."

Franklin and I looked at each other. Franklin cleared his throat. "We owe you an apology, too. I guess we weren't always too understanding. But boy, when you walked into that gun and saved our lives, that was something."

Ian looked pleased. "He wouldn't have fired at us though, you know."

"You didn't know that then," I said. "We think you were very brave."

"And fast!" Franklin said. "Were you ever trained for the Army or anything?"

"I was with Her Majesty's Fusiliers for four years." He smiled, the old half-apologetic smile. "In my salad days."

Mother had said nothing all this time, but she was looking very pleased. Now she said, "I suppose we shall have to cut short our stay here. It doesn't seem quite tactful to go on hanging around. I'd like to suggest that we spend a few days on holiday in New Orleans, then look for another rental, maybe something less isolated this time." She stretched like a contented cat. "I for one want dinner at Brennan's. And I want to wander in the Royal Street antique shops. We could perhaps find a good old-timey Dixieland group in the evening, if there are any good ones left. And the Cabildo. The Cabildo is full of marvelous things, including Napoleon's death mask."

Franklin gave her a warm smile. "There's nothing like a good old death mask to cheer everybody up."

Ian laughed. "I suggest that you girls work out your own itinerary, while Franklin and I track down the haunts of Jean Lafitte. There's the Absinthe House, where he supposedly hung out—"

"With Dominique You." Franklin's eyes were shining.

"And there's the house where he's supposed to have lived . . ."

"I didn't know the English knew about Jean Lafitte," Franklin said.

Ian smiled. "When our friends are interested in something, sometimes we make a point of boning up, don't you know. To share it with them."

"That's really super," Franklin said.

I looked at my mother. She was getting that broad smile that makes a dimple at the corner of her mouth. She said to me softly, "Hello."

And I said, "Hello, Mom."